ARTHUR
MACHEN

The Border Lines Series

Series Editor: John Powell Ward

Elizabeth Barrett Browning	Barbara Dennis
Bruce Chatwin	Nicholas Murray
The Dymock Poets	Sean Street
Edward Elgar: *Sacred Music*	John Allison
Eric Gill & David Jones *at Capel-y-Ffin*	Jonathan Miles
A.E. Housman	Keith Jebb
Francis Kilvert	David Lockwood
Arthur Machen	Mark Valentine
Wilfred Owen	Merryn Williams
Edith Pargeter: *Ellis Peters*	Margaret Lewis
Dennis Potter	Peter Stead
Philip Wilson Steer	Ysanne Holt
Henry Vaughan	Stevie Davies
Mary Webb	Gladys Mary Coles
Samuel Sebastian *Wesley*	Donald Hunt
Raymond Williams	Tony Pinkney

ARTHUR MACHEN

Mark Valentine

Border Lines Series Editor
John Powell Ward

seren

seren is the book imprint of
Poetry Wales Press Ltd
Wyndham Street, Bridgend,
Mid Glamorgan, CF31 1EF
Wales

A CIP record for this book is available at the
British Library Cataloguing in Publication Data Office

ISBN 1-85411-123-X
1-85411-126-4 paperback

*The publisher acknowledges the financial support of the
Arts Council of Wales*

Cover illustration:
Arthur Machen at the Roman Fort, Caerleon

Printed in Palatino by
WBC Book Manufacturers, Bridgend

Contents

List of Illustrations

One: Here Begin Terrors

Sir Arthur Conan Doyle called him a genius: John Betjeman affirmed that his work had changed his life; he has inspired a firmament of composers, musicians, film-makers, mystics and novelists. He wrote what most scholars agree is the greatest horror story ever, and he once made thousands believe that angels had come to earth. He wrote with gusto about beer and tobacco and good company: he also wrote with delicacy about pagan gods, dark fairies and the Holy Grail. He translated Casanova, then turned to fiction after dining with Oscar Wilde: critics have credited him with creating the most beautiful book in the English language, and also, separately, with the most disagreeable one.

Arthur Machen was a man of Gwent, that borderland between England and Wales that was for him also a borderland between this world and another world of wonder and strangeness. He peopled his home town of Caerleon with dream-Romans in their torchlit taverns and marbled gardens: he turned an old white mansion on a hill into the crucible of a devilish experiment; he saw wizened dwarfs and wild gods in the hills and deep woods and labyrinthine lanes of the country around.

He was born in 1863: the year that Thackeray died, the year of George Eliot's *Romola* (which he detested) and Sheridan Le Fanu's *The House by the Churchyard*. When he died, in 1947, the Cheshire-born Malcolm Lowry's symbolist epic *Under the Volcano* had just been published. In a literary career spanning sixty years, Machen achieved passing notoriety twice, but popular appreciation of his books, never. An American critic has evoked some creature of the undead to describe his posthumous fame — he 'will always suffer the indignity of periodic resurrection' (SJ 39 1990) and there have indeed been three revivals of his work, none enduring, though his present literary epiphany is a decade strong.

Virtually all that we know of Machen's childhood and youth is what he chooses to reveal in his yearning, lyrical memoir *Far Off Things* (1922). He was the only son to a line of 'Welsh priests and scholars', as he resonantly put it. His great-grandfather, Daniel Jones, was a curate at St Fagan's, Cardiff, and his grandfather, also Daniel, was vicar of Caerleon for twenty-six years until his death in 1857. His father John Edward Jones followed in the family tradition and took a degree in Divinity at Jesus College, Oxford, leading to an appointment as curate of Alfreton, Derbyshire. On the death of his father, the vicar at Caerleon, John was curate there for a while until he was made vicar of Llanddewi Fach, five miles north-west of Caerleon. He married Janet Machen, the daughter of a naval captain from Greenock, Scotland, who was himself half Welsh. Machen's father added his wife's name to his own in compliance with the terms of a will of one of her family, so that the family became Jones-Machen. Although he dropped the 'Jones' early in adulthood, Machen always remained proudest of the paternal side of his ancestry. In his novel *The Great Return* (1915), a character reproaches Machen as narrator with the glory of a notable forebear:

> your great-grand-uncle Hezekiah, ffeiriad coch yr Castletown — the Red Priest of Castletown — was a great man with the Methodists in his day, and the people flocked by their thousands when he administered the Sacrament. I was born and brought up in Glamorganshire, and old men have wept as they told me of the weeping and contrition that there was when the Red Priest broke the Bread and raised the Cup.

Machen's grandmother and great-aunts were alive during his childhood. We may reasonably assume he heard these sentiments from his own family and he could hardly have helped comparing the greatness of his ancestor to the reduced and forlorn figure of his father, who had an insignificant and unfrequented parish. Though without ambition in the commercial sense, knowledge of a lineage so proud and so fervent must have fired Machen's zeal to make of literature a calling as profound and as passionate.

Machen was born in his grandmother's house, 33 Bridge Street, the main street of Caerleon, on the village square. His parents moved to Llanddewi Fach rectory, newly built on the slopes above the small, narrow church, in the following year; his father's initials, carved in stone near the entrance, may still be seen today, though the house has long since passed from the Church into private ownership. There is no village of Llanddewi Fach as such. It is a scattered parish of farms, small holdings and remote cottages, and even though it was joined with the neighbouring and similar parish of Llandegveth, the living was always poor. Yet, except at the last, the family kept servants and could afford holidays as far afield as Ireland and Guernsey, and the general situation may best be summarised in the phrase 'shabby genteel'. But the worsening poverty of the parishioners, virtually all working in agriculture, came to a head with the great 'smash' of 1880, and his father was forced to declare bankruptcy. From when he was seven years old, whether downtrodden by the descent or not, Machen's mother was a chronic invalid. Both parents were to die before Machen had passed his early twenties.

Yet if this suggests that Machen's childhood was unhappy, that does not give a true picture, for he found two great consolations, literature and nature. He described his life until the age of seventeen as all 'solitude and woods and deep lanes and wonder' and he early adopted the habit of wandering on long walks in the Gwent countryside around his home. It was his meditations on the ancient, often hidden, places he visited that made him long to turn them into stories. 'I shall always esteem it as the greatest piece of fortune that has fallen to me', he wrote, 'that I was born in that noble, fallen Caerleon-on-Usk, in the heart of Gwent ... anything which I may have accomplished in literature is due to the fact that when my eyes were first opened in earliest childhood they had before them the vision of an enchanted land' (*Far Off Things*, Chapter 1, 1922).

It is a land bounded by mountains, which Machen reverently names as if they were the great deities of a classical myth: 'Twyn Barlwm, that mystic tumulus', 'Mynydd Maen, the Mountain of the Stone', 'the pointed summit of the holy mountain by Abergavenny ... a pure blue in the far sunshine'. And within this domain, the young Machen soon became a familiar of all the secret and ageless places.

Gwent is an ancient Celtic principality which only finally succumbed to alien rule during the Norman conquests. It mostly became the English county of Monmouthshire. Its borders delineated by rivers, including the Wye and the mouth of the Severn, and watered at its heart by the 'tawny Usk' in its 'mystic, winding esses' (as Machen conjured it) and the Soar brook, it is a realm of arcadian loveliness only marginally spoiled by modern urban development around its principal town of Newport and to the west, Pontypool and Ebbw Vale. Although he left Gwent in his early years, seldom ever to return, Machen was never other than a fervent son of his own land. If he visited it with terrors and enchantments, it was because he was inspired by its beauty and richness, not out of any hostility.

Forty years after he left it, Machen was still proud of the town of his birth and could write lyrically of its legends and its loneliness:

> I am a citizen of what was once no mean city ... this city is Caerleon-on-Usk, once the splendid Isca Silurum, the head-quarters of the Second Augustan Legion. And, then again, a golden mist of legend grew about it; it became the capital of King Arthur's court of faerie and enchantment, the chief city of a cycle of romance that has charmed all the world. I remember it as it was fifty-six years ago: dreaming in the sun by the yellow Usk, as it always seemed to me; its streets all silent, so that a rare footstep echoed in them and people came to their windows and doorsteps to spy out who the stranger might be. It was all white, set in its level meadows by the river, the hills fencing it about, and northwards there appeared the wooded heights and slopes of Wentwood, 'quivering with leaves, very conspicuous'. A wonderful town for all that it was such a tiny place; and wonderful was it to stand in the evening on the green circle of the Roman amphitheatre, and see the sun flame above Twyn Barlwm, the mystic tumulus on the mountain wall of the west. So the old town dreamed the long years away, not forgetful of the Legions and the Eagles, murmuring scraps of broken Latin in its ancient sleep, speaking of a certain bridge, as Pont Sadwrn (Pons Saturni), and of the hamlet across the river as Caerleon-ultra-Pontem.
>
> (Introduction to *Notes and Queries*, 1926)

But second only to his love of this home domain were his explorations in his father's rambling library where he read eagerly the books that were to form his character as much as the lonely pilgrimages in the country. In *Far Off Things* he glories in the treasured tomes he remembered — *The Arabian Nights, Don Quixote*, Tennyson, Parker's *Glossary of Gothic Architecture, Wuthering Heights*, George Borrow, Sir Walter Scott. Here too were bound volumes of distinguished journals, *Chambers', Cornhill, The Welcome Guest*, and Dickens's *Household Words*, with its singularly well-informed series of essays on alchemy, which so fired the young man's imagination. Later, too, there were the stranger characters of English literature, Sir Thomas Browne, William Hazlitt and Thomas De Quincey, whose prose was all carven and curious with twisting simile and gilded metaphor. From the ages of eleven to seventeen, Machen was a boarder at Hereford Cathedral School, which he describes merely as 'an interlude among strangers', for he was already 'set to loneliness'. He was later savagely to satirise public schools in his romance *The Secret Glory* (1922) but this attack seems to have had origins other than his own schooldays. Certainly he acknowledged the influence of his school on his decision to become a writer.

The school is an ancient foundation situated in the Cathedral close a little way from the High Street of what is a quiet, medium-sized market town, not a city in the great urban sense at all. During Machen's time there were about fifty boarders. In his old age, writing for an American readership, Machen characterised the finest possible education in terms which make it clear he was thinking of Hereford:

> You must go to school in an ancient town; rather, if it can be managed, in an ancient cathedral city. I will not say that cloisters are absolutely indispensable, but if they may be had, it will certainly be very much the better. A quiet green quadrangle, a close within a close, will do a great deal of good, and there should be grey walls about these green still places, and late fifteenth century stone mullioned windows looking out on them, and behind these walls and windows the abodes of Priests Vicars, or Vicars Choral, or Minor Canons.
>
> Gardens, where peaches ripen on old red walls, slope down to the river; the mystical mount of the cathedral rises above all; and somewhere in a nook near all these delights, is the old grammar school built itself of old stone, founded five hundred years ago ... To such a school, thus girt about with beauty and peace, you must go when you are ten years old or thereabouts, and for the next eight or nine years you must devote yourself to Latin and Greek and to very little else.
>
> (SS 221 1995)

This recollection, fifty years later and perhaps a little hallowed by the passing of time, nonetheless shows that Machen was more impressed by his schooldays than the reticence of his autobiography suggests, and this period may well have been highly formative in establishing his later unchanging beliefs about religion, society and art. The devotion to the sanctity and mystery of the Mass, so fervently described in several of his writings, is more likely to have been inspired by the cathedral services he attended as a schoolboy than those of his father in the rather sparse church at Llanddewi. His traditionalism, which later led him to point out that the most contented place in the British Isles was the feudal seigneurity of Guernsey, must have been significantly suggested in youth by the ordered serenity of the cathedral's ceremonial round. But he defended the school against the suggestion that it was privileged:

> My old grammar school was very much far from being exclusive. The boys were the sons of county parsons, of doctors, lawyers, squireens, farmers, and the town tradesmen. It was not that the grocer and the ironmonger wanted 'to turn their sons into gentlemen'. In two instances that I remember, the lads went cheerfully from Sophocles to the shop. The ironmonger, I recollect, was especially anxious that his boy should become an elegant Latin versifier. The grocer's son was somewhat to seek in this art, and I did the elegiacs for him; my fee being a pound of Roquefort cheese.
> (SS 222 1995)

Machen concluded this valedictory essay on 'The Old Grammar School' with the comment that it was 'a good, sober, altogether English thing ... it had no proud looks, nor windy pretensions' and indeed none of his contemporaries achieved even his own degree of public eminence, though many took holy orders, which could only have made more pointed his involuntary desertion from the time-honoured vocation of his family. John Walmsley (1867-1922), four years Machen's junior, became Bishop of Sierra Leone, while an almost exact contemporary, Alfred York Browne (1861-1906) was military chaplain at Bombay and Aden.

We know that Machen did well at the school, leading the lists in Classics and Divinity, but his time there may also have been dogged by his father's poverty. Indeed, his absence for a few months could have been due to this, and it may be that this is why he did not make much of his schooldays directly in his work. However, he is recorded as attending one of the annual Old Herefordian dinners in 1923, perhaps significantly when his literary reputation was at its highest, and he supplied an entry about his career for a school history in 1931, so that we may infer that his affection for the school grew in his later years, when the memory of the hardships had mellowed.

When he left school it was not at all clear what his career should be and the family's impoverishment meant that the question was pressing. There was no money to send him to university to get the degree necessary to enter the Church. At first there was some thought that he might go into medicine, and he went up to London to take the examination for the Royal College of Surgeons: but he failed owing to his complete incapacity for arithmetic.

But his composition of a long poem on the Greek Mysteries, *Eleusinia*, led his family to think (by somewhat ingenuous reasoning, surely) that he might make a journalist. The poem, privately published at a local stationer in an edition of one hundred (1881) is now a book collector's talisman, searched for since the 1920s. The precise number of copies known still to exist has never been certain. It is at least two, and may be as many as four. This blank verse juvenilia is of no great merit, as Machen and all his followers frankly concede, but its significance is in its origin and its relationship to the rest of his work. For in a later essay about the poem, 'Beneath the Barley' (1931), Machen recalled his 'indescribable emotion' at the land before him on a walk one day in the autumn of 1880. Literature, he averred, 'is the art of describing the indescribable; the art of exhibiting symbols which may hint at the ineffable mysteries behind them; the art of the veil, which reveals what it conceals'. And so, no matter how great the fall from what he saw that day, the mountains 'a pure, radiant blue', the whitewashed walls of farm cottages shining like marble, to what he was able to write to celebrate that vision, nevertheless, as he claimed, 'I chose the mysteries first and I chose them last'.

There were other reasons why he might make a writer than simply the promise of this classical poem. Machen identifies three: 'as a man three parts Celt, I was by nature inclined to the work of words'; 'the heredity of bookishness ... from grandfathers and uncles and cousins' and 'the old-fashioned grammar school education ... an education in words'. But Machen consistently held true to the Romantic idea of the writer's special calling.

Speculating again, in a letter to an American admirer in 1924, as to what made him become a writer, Machen wrote:

> I look back as you ask me, look back forty-three years and more, and look at that poor boy wandering and loafing and

mooning about the lanes and fields near Llanddewi Fach Rectory. Had this poor wretch a choice set before him: leather and comfort or literature and misery?

The answer is: not for one moment.

For in the first place; there is not the faintest trace of the business faculty in my character. I am the son, grandson, great grandson of Welsh priests and scholars; and not one of them knew or understood or cared anything about the commercial life. Such a career never even occurred to me; I no more thought of it than I think now, at 61, of learning to be an acrobat.

And then, on the other hand ... I never thought of literature as a career. I never said to myself on the one hand:

'Literature is a vilely paid business, except for the success-ful few. But perhaps I shall be one of the successful few'. I never calculated the matter at all, or acknowledged the chances of the future, either as to praise or pudding. Literature — I quote again from myself — was not a career, but a destiny. I felt within me a fervent desire to write. There is no rational explanation of this desire; it was more like the instinct of a bird or a beetle than the reasoned scheme of a man.

(AFL 23 1993)

But from June 1881 to December 1882 he prepared himself for journalism, partly in practical matters such as learning shorthand, but mostly by reading more and more, becoming by turns absorbed in the *Mabinogion*, the collection of Celtic folk tales, Boswell's *Life of Dr Johnson*, William Morris's *The Earthly Paradise* and the poems of Robert Herrick, which 'brought me into the seventeenth century, into an age which I have loved ever since with a peculiar devotion'.

At this time he moved to London and 'Here Begin Terrors' said Machen in *Far Off Things*, characteristically citing the medieval romance the *Grand Saint Graal* to sum up his years of privation and struggle in the city, living in a narrow garret room in Clarendon Road and sustained mostly by dry bread, green tea and quantities of shag tobacco. It was a time of penury and isolation, during which he got work where he could, as a junior in a publisher's office, and as a private tutor, and spent his free time wandering in London as he had in his home country, shocked and morbidly compelled by the squalor and crudity of the surroundings.

Journalist's work proved initially hard to obtain, but, true to his relish for the recondite, Machen's literary career began to take substance when the publisher George Redway agreed to put out, in

1884, his *The Anatomy of Tobacco*, a quaint celebration of the joys of smoking, done in imitation of Robert Burton's *The Anatomy of Melancholy* (1621), that huge, humour-riddled wedge of philosophy, folklore, classic Jacobean physick and much else. Machen honoured this book as 'a great refuge ... a world of literature in itself', and called his own work 'a grave burlesque of what I loved'.

His pastiche is still diverting today and it was several times quarried for quotations in the days when smoking anthologies were still a permissible thing for a publisher to do, but the subject is not deep enough to sustain interest over more than eighty pages, as Machen acknowledged: 'it was all too elaborate, elephantine, prolonged'.

When the book was nearly done, Machen experienced what was to become a familiar descent into a quiet despondency, at his inability to capture what he really wanted to convey. Again and again, he felt the book that he had finished was not the book it should have been, and this anguish at the chasm between the idea and the reality shows also in the discarded novels, the cancelled chapters and the unwritten works which litter his career. 'We dream in fire, and we work in clay' was his memorable summary of the artist's torture, and at the close of chapter five of *Far Off Things*, describing the *Anatomy*, he made this very failure itself into a poetic image: 'There was a wild sunset, scarlet and green and gold, and as it were, gardens of Persian roses, far in the evening sky. I stood by an old twisted oak, and thought of my book as I would have made it, and sighed, and so went home and made it as I could'.

Redway not rising to Machen's suggestions for further original work, the young author agreed to undertake the first complete translation of *The Heptameron*, the amatory tales of Marguerite, Queen of Navarre, that Renaissance woman who was the patron of Erasmus, and many other men of letters, and the fountainhead of a court of sparkling learning and humanist thought. Machen employed a vigorous, variegated vocabulary to convey the majesty and merriment of the original work, using that seventeenth century pastiche he had achieved so well for the *Anatomy*. For a young man who had barely attained his majority, the translation is a veritable *tour de force*. It is not much admired by modern translators, who object to the archaic language, but it was not finally superseded for over seventy years. For Machen the book was always of happy memory since to write it he had returned home, to the rectory of

Llanddewi, where he could wander again in the old deep lanes and among the ruined houses and wild gardens of 'undiscovered lands'. Yet, as he said, 'there seemed nothing to do next,' until the summer of 1885 when Redway offered him a miscellaneous sort of employment, and it was necessary for him to return to the dreary cell in Clarendon Road where he had suffered of old.

The work was mainly the cataloguing of a vast collection of esoteric works on the occult. If Machen's reading had previously been in out-of-the-way literature, this experience only steeped him even more deeply in strange knowledge, for he was called upon to dip into, and give some description of, each book. This period yielded another Machen oddity, his pastiche of a 'lost' chapter from *Don Quijote*, used to advertise Redway's catalogue, with references to such luminaries as Thomas Taylor, the parson Platonist; the alchemist Thomas Vaughan, twin of the metaphysical poet Henry; the prophet Nostradamus, the mystic Behren, the astrologer William Lilly, and a tantalising array of other workers in the fields of hermeticism, herbalism, freemasonry, divination, and the pagan faith.

In the autumn of 1885, at the end of this work for Redway, and once again in poverty, Machen began to dream of writing a Great Romance, a work that would celebrate his beloved Gwent. Yet he found that the vision he had for the book would not become more corporeal, it remained intangible and misty. He wrote the Dedication and the Epilogue and in an almost macabre flourish romanticised his present destitution in gracious, courtly language as a voyage to the Isle of Farre Joyaunce, rather than the workhouse which more surely loomed for him. But by a singular stroke, the next post brought a summons back to Gwent in November 1885, where his mother had just died.

In the rectory, then, with his disconsolate father, Machen wrote his first work of fiction, *The Chronicle of Clemendy*. While 'the winter rains scoured the land ... I wrote on in the silent house; struggling against the bitter conviction of my incapacity'.

Machen had become so accustomed to working with archaic language, in his translation and in his delving into ancient grimoires, that he simply continued in the same vein in his original writings. But this work was also influenced by his reading. Machen acknowledged its origins as 'a great delight in Rabelais the unreachable, Balzac's *Contes Drolatiques* [1837: first English translation, 1874], and in my own country, Gwent'. The book is a series of tales told by a company of friends who form a noble order of ale-quaffers with such titles as the Lord Maltworm and the Tankard Marshall, and who journey to a great festival at the town of Usk. Their tales are of lusty knights, fair ladies and merry monks, and nearly all are set in the Gwent region: we may trace their progress to Abergavenny, Caerleon, the forest of Wentwood, Caldicot Castle and elsewhere: justly does Machen call his book 'the Silurian Mythologies', after the geological name for the region.

The Chronicle of Clemendy, for all its quaintness, can still be enjoyed today. It has gusto, good humour, and a gentle grace in the telling. In its mingling of an epicurean delight in the table and the tankard and the tobacco bowl, and a relish for improbable yarns, it is in the same good company as Thomas Love Peacock's novels, and its amiable bachelors are distinctly Pickwickian too. There is even a hint of the flavour of Jerome's Three Men in a Boat (1889), which was to become so popular in the year after Clemendy was published: Jerome was to become a good friend of Machen.

Machen's romance did not, however, attract such public attention. Though medievalism had been a continued refrain in Victorian culture, from the novels of Sir Walter Scott to the paintings of the Pre-Raphelites, it was a drawing-room medievalism of chivalry and romantic quests, not the earthier version Machen knew from the authentic texts of the time. Even had his work received attention, the slightly risqué tone could well have caused disquiet. As it was, its author was unknown, it was privately published, and reviewers, with one notable exception, ignored it. The exception was the respected French critic Octave Uzanne, who acclaimed it in Le Livre as 'le renouveau de la Renaissance'. Machen remarked, with ironic deference, 'I am surrendering my judgement wholly to that of Mr Octave Uzanne'.

Thirty years later, Machen's American champion Vincent Starrett praised Clemendy equally highly:

> It is the Welsh Heptameron, a chronicle of amorous intrigue, joyous drunkenness, and knightly endeavour second to none in the brief muster of the world's great classics ... Machen proves himself the peer of either [Balzac and Boccaccio] in gay, irresponsible, diverting, unflagging invention, while his diction is lovelier than that of any of his forerunners ...
> (VS 30-1 1918)

Yet the book has also been reviled even by Machen enthusiasts, some calling it 'unreadable', while others have criticised it for being too long and insufficiently bawdy to bear comparison with its fore-bears.

Clemendy's true worth surely lies somewhere between these two extremes. The acclaim is much more than can justly be sustained: the complaints are too severe. It is a pleasant book, a fine curio, and one which will always win the allegiance of connoisseurs in obscure literature, but it is not a significant work even in the Machen canon and it will never be widely read.

The year 1887 was a momentous one for Machen. In August, he married Amy Hogg, a bohemian woman some thirteen years his senior, and the couple both modified their ages for the official documentation of the wedding, so that the age difference was more conventional. We know virtually nothing about Machen's first wife except her family background: Machen does not directly mention her in his autobiographies at all. We do not know how they met or how long they courted, but Jerome K. Jerome, in his memoirs (JKJ 1926) recalled that Amy was strongly involved in theatrical circles, and lived alone in 'diggings' near the British Museum: either of these circumstances could have led the couple to make each other's acquaintance. Amy came from a colonial family who had lived mostly in Bengal before retiring to Worthing, Sussex. Jerome empha-sises her independence and unconventionality. In a letter to Harry Spurr, co-publisher of *Clemendy*, Machen recounts with relish a rambling holiday with Amy a month before their marriage, an unusual arrangement for the time: '... we have tramped about hill and dale, by mountains and river through this delicious land to our heart's content. We have tasted of the native beverage cwrw dda [beer], as also of seidr [cider]: we have drunk from holy wells and the mountain torrents, we have laughed, sung and joked in a thor-oughly Silurian manner ...' (SL 212 1988).

Godfrey Brangham, in an unpublished study, has pointed out that virtually all of Machen's prime work was written during the period of his marriage to Amy, and that she 'glides ghost-like through the paragraphs and pages of his works', especially in the characters of the beautiful young women in *A Fragment of Life* (1904) and 'The Rose Garden' (1897). Her influence on Machen must always remain truly incalculable. Amy died of cancer in 1899 after an illness which lasted for half the length of their marriage.

Scarcely a month after his marriage, Machen's father died and his last link with the area he loved had been severed. He began to receive small family inheritances which eased his financial straits, though there was still the need to earn a living. For the next three years, living with his wife in Great Russell Street, close to the British Museum, Machen worked as a cataloguer, translator and at last, as a journalist, when he began to contribute reviews to *Walford's Antiquarian* journal and later, his own work to an assortment of other periodicals. The reviews show Machen as still immersed in the esoteric, for the books he examined included such titles as *Syrian Stone-Lore, Phantasms of the Living*, and *The Gnostics and Their Remains*. Machen also made his own characteristic contributions, with essays on 'The Curiosities of Ale' and 'The Allegorical Significance of the Tinctures in Heraldry'.

The same year saw the publication of what Machen called a 'drawing-room' edition of *The Heptameron*, with an introduction by A. Mary F. Robinson which he characterised as 'elaborate and very tiresome'. This new version, under the title *The Fortunate Lovers*, omits some of the racier tales.

Machen's cataloguing work for another bookseller had also led to a new translating commission, *The Memoirs of Jacques Casanova*, a substantial work of over five thousand pages, which took him a year to complete, often working at home in his drab rooms, and on very modest pay. By the time his employers were ready to publish the twelve volume set, in 1894, Machen's finances were much healthier owing to family legacies, and he invested some money in the undertaking. His translation proved popular, and has been reprinted over seventeen times. Machen remained quietly proud of his achievement, supplying new prefaces to three subsequent editions. The combination of improbable adventures, courtliness and erotic intrigue appealed to Machen, who characterised the book as 'vastly entertaining', and he gave serious thoughts to Casanova's significance in literature and as a chronicler of eighteenth century modes. If he had done nothing else, this translation would remain a monument to Machen's literary zeal.

However, Machen's appetite for bizarre literature had not been assuaged, and he began on his own account to translate Beroalde de Verville's *Le Moyen de Parvenir*, that 'extraordinary and enigmatic book' as he calls it, a Rabelaisian gargoyle of a work which printers refused to handle in its proper state, so that he was obliged to issue only an edited version, *Fantastic Tales* (1889). He had come upon the book while cataloguing for Robinson and Kerlake, the Casanova booksellers, and found himself unable simply to sample the book in order to describe it; he had to read it. Young people, he later remarked, 'think more of the gargoyles grinning on the parapet than of the aspiration of the spire' and so it was with this book. De Verville, a seventeenth century canon of Tours, wrote 'many dull and improving books' but it is for this work he has his place in literature. Machen's translation is certainly an unusual accomplishment for a young man and it is lively enough to be diverting reading today for lovers of the bizarre, but when he was later (in 1930) asked to undertake a fuller translation, he passed the commission to a younger friend, Oliver Stonor, and contented himself with writing the introduction.

In 1890 Machen returned to fiction when he began to contribute to several periodicals, including the *Globe, Whirlwind* and *St James Gazette.* He began by writing essays and articles, but in the summer of that year he sent Oscar Wilde a copy of *Fantastic Tales* because he had read some remark of the fashionable playwright which made him think he would appreciate such a strange book. An invitation to dine followed, and Wilde outlined to Machen a story by a friend which he praised highly. Machen thought he could better this and so, with Wilde's encouragement, turned to society tales, initially rather slight. His interest in the singular, however, soon surfaced, as did the sort of amorous intrigue he had found in the translations he undertook.

Machen's only detailed recollection of his acquaintance with Wilde was recorded thirty-five years later in a letter to an American admirer. It reflects an ambivalent mingling of attraction and repulsion:

> He was not really affected. If I may say so, he affected affectation. He would say ridiculous things, but he expected you to laugh at them, not to take them as prophetic utterances. He would laugh at his own literary poses: thus:
> O.W. 'Did you see that letter in the Telegraph this morning signed "O"?'
> A.M. 'Yes, and I recognised the authorship'.
> O.W. (whimsically) 'Ah, I was afraid it was rather Oscarish'.
> I may say that so far as I knew him there was nothing of depth in his talk. He glided fantastically, whimsically, over the surface of things. His attitude, as it appeared to me, was:

'I know quite well that there are the everlasting problems; but they have nothing to do with me, nor I with them'.

He dined with me once again ... And on this occasion, I do remember being struck with the fact that there was a certain sameness in Wilde's talk. It was not that he repeated himself or said over again the things that he had said before: rather, the mould of his conversation remained the same, the manner was the same, the turns and tricks and quips were all in the one vein. No new mood was indicated, no different angle of vision was manifested. But this, very likely and for all I know, may have been due to the fact that Wilde saw that there was no real sympathy between us, no vital common ground, as it were; and so he set himself to be politely — and delightfully — entertaining in his usual manner.

A year or two after this I again met him accidentally... He was furious. The Lord Chamberlain had refused to license the performance of *Salome* — I think it was *Salome* — even in French, with Mme Sarah Bernhardt in the title-part. The interview between us was brief. There were no quips. He was just an angry man; like any other angry man. And now for the last time. Wilde when I saw him first in 1890 was a man of distinguished appearance. He was not handsome — there was something mis-shapen about his mouth — but he was impressive in a high degree. You said to yourself: 'Here is one who is something and somewhat'. The last time I met him was in 1895; the year of the crash. I had written *The Great God Pan* in the interval, and I had gone to my publisher's on some business. I was shown into a waiting-room where Oscar Wilde and a friend were standing. I believe Wilde's libel action had already begun, or was at all events in the cause-list, for the publisher apologized to me for having had me shown into the same room as Wilde and his friend: 'hoped I didn't mind'. But Wilde was a shocking sight. He had become a great mass of rosy fat. His body seemed made of rolls of fat. He was pendulous. He was like nothing but an obese old French-woman, of no extraordinary fame, dressed up in man's clothes. He horrified me. We only had a word or two.

(AFL 29-3, 1993)

The first tale Machen published, 'St. John's Chef' (July 1890: *St James Gazette*) was a trifle, clever but superficial, about a baronet who is his own chef: and there may well have been others of this kind, now undiscovered, since Machen could not recall in later years all the contributions he had made.

But 'A Double Return' (September 1890: anonymous) first marked Machen out. The story caused 'a fluttering in the dovecotes' according to Wilde, because of its theme of accidental adultery. Another, 'A Wonderful Woman' (December 1890: *The Whirlwind*) hinted at the reckless, indiscreet past of a demure wife and could scarcely have been any more welcome to the respectable classes. 'The Iron Maid' (September 1890: *St James Gazette*) could only have strengthened Mrs Grundy's conviction that Machen was not quite acceptable. It is an early macabre piece which tells of a man who collects instruments of torture and death and meets a fitting, if predictable, end. (A rather similar plot was used by Bram Stoker in his story 'The Squaw' (from *Dracula's Guest*, 1914) though here it is more elaborate). These stories may have identified Machen at an early stage with the 'daring' writing coming from the Decadents, that coterie of young bohemian artists and poets who gathered around Wilde and proclaimed the theory of life as artifice and adornment.

Decadence in Britain may be said to have emerged from two main sources. One was the aesthetical philosophy of the 1880s, chiefly articulated by Walter Pater: the other was the French decadent poets such as Verlaine and Mallarme. It began around the time of Wilde's *The Picture of Dorian Gray*, in 1890, and ended but for some lingering devotees with Wilde's imprisonment in 1894. Arthur Symons, a leading spokesman for the movement, conceded the term 'Decadence' was 'rarely used with any precise meaning', but its enemies were sure they knew what it meant. After his downfall, Wilde was condemned by the 'respectable' press as 'the High Priest of the Decadents' who were accused of having 'hideous conceptions of the meaning of art' and 'worse than Eleusinian mysteries', while they were deemed to be against 'all the wholesome, manly, simple ideals of English life' (Quoted by R.K.R. Thornton in *Decadence and the 1890s*, 16, 1979). While there has been no succinct and accurate encapsulation of what the Decadence meant, it may very broadly be considered as implying a devotion to exquisitely crafted style in literature, and in life to the quest for new sensations, involving variously the exploration of the occult, the exotic, the sexually unorthodox, the bohemian way of life, and a taste for strange drugs or drink.

In his later novel, *The Hill of Dreams*, Machen allies himself with the Decadents by wickedly parodying a typical society reviewer, who fulminates against 'the abandoned artist and the scrofulous stylist' preferring 'a faithful reproduction of the open and manly life' (chapter four). The themes of his novels, too, parallel those of the Decadents summarised above. Though he had no time for the emblems of the movement, 'peacocks and lilies and sunflowers' as he summarised them, there is no doubt that his imagination was imbued with the themes associated with the Decadents, implying a deeper familiarity than he ever openly admitted.

In 'The Lost Club', (December 1890: *The Whirlwind*), indeed, Machen's protagonist is a young man described as 'a true son of the carnation' and 'a gorgeous young gentleman', clear references to the dandyism of the Decadents, and their emblem the Green Carnation, adopted by Wilde as a pose to show art improving upon nature. Machen's tale has some obvious similarities to Robert Louis Stevenson's 'The Suicide Club' (1878) but in Machen's story the secret of the mysterious club is never revealed. Its votaries disappear, but they do not die; we do not know what happens to them. According to Machen, the story was 'founded on certain rumours current in London in 1890', though these had a different ending. These were clearly curious enough for Machen to remember them over forty years later when the tale was reprinted, but we shall probably remain in the dark about what was involved. Arthur Conan Doyle used a similar theme, the strange society that suddenly vanishes, in his Sherlock Holmes adventure of the 'Red Headed League' just a few months after Machen's story, but whether he was in any way prompted by it, or by the same rumours, cannot now be said.

All of these early stories, with their hints of the scandalous and bizarre, prepared the way for Machen's first major work, the novel *The Great God Pan*. But at the same time as he wrote these cosmopolitan anecdotes, he contributed quite distinct prose sketches in which there is a different mood altogether, one of reverie and vision, a dwelling upon the splendour of landscape. Again, there may well have been more of these than we now know, for they were by nature fugitive impressions. Four of them have been collected quite recently (*Rus in Urbe and Other Pieces*, Tartarus Press, 1992) and the title piece in particular (*St James's Gazette*: July 1890) represents the first real attempt by Machen to convey the sense of strangeness and wonder he perceived in the Gwent terrain, the theme of much of his later work. The piece begins conventionally enough, on the theme that to the exile from the countryside, the park is but a poor substitute, but Machen's prose quickens when he describes the exile imagining his lost land:

> there is built up the great mountain range, whose huge round
> bastions are clothed with green bracken, from whose stony
> sides pour out so many streams of clear, cold water, the
> sources of many a brook and rivulet; for him flame all the far
> glories of the evening sun sinking into the heart of the tumu-
> lus that crowns the summit of the mountain, the memorial of
> a forgotten people; for him rises the evensong of the river in
> the valley as the wind dies down and the trees are still. Or
> maybe he tracks once more a stream that rushes down from
> boulder to boulder in the midst of a glen in the great hills;
> tracks it by steep wild fields closing in and growing steeper,
> by over-hanging gleaming birches, by thick woods of beech
> stunted by the winter winds and gnarled and twisted into all
> manner of fantastic shapes ...

This intrusion of the sinister, the misshapen trees, in an otherwise
idyllic evocation, strikes the keynote for Machen's later treatment of
a landscape which seems to be imbued with active, brooding evil.
Yet it is a land which can also be steeped in a sacred splendour.

There is a clear separation between these pastoral poems-in-prose
and the outré tales of men about town and their strange experiences.
Yet each represents an aspect of his first real novel, *The Great God
Pan*, in which the two elements fuse, and we find his foppish youths
plunged into a mystery which arises from the remote fastness of
mystic Gwent, a mystery that was to make Machen's name and
identify him ever after as a master of the macabre.

Two: Sacraments of Evil

The first chapter of *The Great God Pan* was originally a separate story, 'The Experiment', written in Summer 1890 and published in *The Whirlwind* the following December. In January 1891 Machen began another story, 'The City of Resurrections', but soon realised that what he was writing was really a continuation of the earlier tale, and that a longer work could be devised: as he hoped, it would be 'a curious and beautiful thing'. But the idea that had come to him refused to be conveyed on the page, and he wrote only 'with horrid difficulty, with sick despairs' and even then could not find a final chapter until June of that year, when the book was completed. He tried various publishers until the work was accepted, after several alterations suggested by the reader, by John Lane at the Bodley Head, then one of the most fashionable publishers. A second story, 'The Inmost Light' was added to the volume. The book was published in December 1894 and caused an immediate furore, which Machen was apt later to play down a little, though he did concede it prompted a minor scandal, and recalled Oscar Wilde complimenting him on 'un grand succes'. Almost uniquely amongst Machen's books, *The Great God Pan* reached enough of a popular readership to require an immediate second edition.

It is not a long work, what is now called a novella, about ninety pages in all, in eight parts, and it has two technical weaknesses which can deter a casual reader. It is structured as a set of separate episodes which ultimately are seen to interlock and inform one another, but until this connection becomes clear there is an impression of fragmentation, of lack of focus. And it describes the activities of various gentlemen who each play some part in the story but do not have distinctive characters, so that it is possible to become confused by the role of each. But though these deficiencies have been seized on by later critics, they were not what exercised the minds of contemporaries, who were sufficiently enraged or enraptured by its subject matter.

In the hush of dusk in a house in the West, suspended between a great forest and a winding river, Dr Raymond, a student of 'transcendental medicine', has summoned his friend Clarke to witness an experiment on a young girl, his ward. A minor incision in certain nerve cells will, the doctor believes, break down the barrier between this world, and another of which we know little. On the surface, the operation is surgical, a work of physiological vivisection; but Machen's evocation of the scene has more in common with an alchemical experiment. In his essay 'Sorcery and Sanctity: the Spagyric Quest of Arthur Machen', Ron Weighell draws attention to the moment when Clarke waits for Dr Raymond to begin; 'An odour in the air acts upon his senses like a drug, inducing the vision of a grove in which he confronts a presence "neither man nor beast, neither the living nor the dead, but all things mingled".' He points out that 'The use of perfumes ... to create an atmosphere conducive to visions of the relevant deity, is a magical technique based on the theory of cabalistic correspondence' (A & M 13 1986).

Machen explained his ambiguous description of the operation in a letter to his publisher in March 1894:

> If I were writing in the Middle Ages I should need no scientific basis ... In these days the supernatural per se is entirely incredible; to believe, we must link our wonders to some scientific or pseudo-scientific fact, or basis, or method. Thus we do not believe in 'ghosts' but in telepathy, not in 'witchcraft' but in hypnotism. If Mr Stevenson had written his great masterpiece about 1590-1650, Dr Jekyll would have made a compact with the devil. In 1886 Dr Jekyll sends to the Bond Street chemists for some rare drugs'.
> (SL 218 1988)

This reference to Robert Louis Stevenson's *The Strange Case of Dr Jekyll and Mr Hyde* (1886) is significant because Machen's book was perceived and received partly in the shadow of this macabre classic. *The Pall Mall Gazette*, for example, saw *The Great God Pan* as a straight successor: 'Since Mr Stevenson played with the crucibles of science in *Dr Jekyll and Mr Hyde* we have not encountered a more successful experiment of the sort', and the *Glasgow Herald* concurred; 'Nothing more striking or more skilful than this book has been produced in the way of what one may call Borderland fiction since Mr Stevenson's ... *Dr Jekyll and Mr Hyde'*.

Stevenson (1850-1894) was by this time living in Samoa in the vain hope of resisting his tuberculosis, but his work had a signal impact upon many younger writers of the period. He was admired both for the seriousness with which he treated the craft of writing and his ability to tell a good story in a vivid, nimble style remote from the ponderousness of most of his contemporaries. Richard Le Gallienne recalled that Stevenson's essays were always read 'with a great respect and admiration' by the younger writers of the nineties (*The Romantic Nineties*, 1926). Stevenson had first come to notice with his travel writings and essays between 1879-82, a reputation fostered by the sprightly extravaganza *New Arabian Nights* (1882) and the adventure yarn *Treasure Island* (1883). But it was *Jekyll and Hyde* that made his fame, turning him into a cult figure both in Britain and America, and it is little wonder that this was the nearest point of reference in literature for both the critics and Machen himself, when considering *The Great God Pan*: those who made the comparison to Stevenson were indeed bestowing high praise.

The effect of the experiment on the girl Mary is inevitable, and it is sketched by Machen in two simple paragraphs. We see her awake with a shudder of ecstasy which at once is replaced by convulsive terror: later we learn she has become a hopeless idiot. It has sometimes been said that it is a shame Machen ever did add to this single episode, and it is undeniably effective: but the succeeding chapters take us into stranger terrain still and bring in the extra twist which was most to offend Victorian sensibility.

In the second chapter, we meet Mr Clarke many years later when he is a bachelor scholar for whom 'lust always prevailed' — but the lust is for his collection of documents on 'the most morbid subjects', which he is compiling into his 'Memoirs to Prove the Existence of the Devil'. A friend, Dr Phillips, has written him an account of two sinister episodes in the life of Helen Vaughan, a girl in the Welsh border country, in which she seems to lure children into corrupting encounters in the deep forest. The dim shadow of the faun begins to move into our cognizance.

Chapter three, which Machen began as a separate story, introduces new characters. Villiers, an idler about town, encounters an old college friend Herbert, who has become a ragged beggar. Visiting an acquaintance, Austin, he learns that this descent was due to a marriage to a woman of sordid depravity, linked with an unsolved murder. We sense there was something more than a figure of speech when Herbert told Villiers she corrupted him 'body and soul'.

While Villiers begins to delve further, Austin receives a portfolio of drawings done by an artist friend, Arthur Meyrick, who has died aged thirty, 'a frightful Walpurgis-night of evil, strange monotonous evil ... set forth in hard black and white. The figures of fauns and satyrs and Aegipars danced before his eyes'. On one page there is a portrait of Mrs Herbert. It is curious that this evocation of an artist in diabolism must have been written before Aubrey Beardsley began his audacious designs featuring leering satyrs, cynical fauns and orgiastic figures, before the boy whom Roger Fry called the 'Fra Angelico of Satanism' had even been widely published.

The reader now suspects that the sinister Mrs Herbert is responsible for the ruin of at least two men. Chapter four quickens the pace of her infamies by reporting a string of mysterious suicides by aristocrats and gentlemen. The investigative Villiers establishes that this woman and the Welsh girl (of chapter two) are one person and, with Clarke and a physician, he visits this femme fatale and forces her suicide.

Dr Matheson, the third one present, records his experience in a Latin manuscript. Amid an odour of corruption, he sees the woman's form begin to melt and dissolve, 'waver from sex to sex,' 'descend to the beasts' and end as 'a substance like jelly' before the entry into the unnatural blackness of the room of 'a Form,' the symbol of which — but not, note, the reality — can be seen in ancient sculptures and paintings. Clarke makes contact with Dr Raymond again and learns that Helen Vaughan/Mrs Herbert was the daughter of Mary, born to her nine months after the experiment they witnessed. And the father? Machen does not need to say it directly.

Whom the gods love ... Machen has taken a classical tradition, and pushed it to the extremes. The loves of Apollo do not end well, nor often the loves of Zeus, and as for Pan, we need only consider the fatoe of Pityr (turned into a pine), Syrinx (the reed) and Echo.

Yet these transformations are more poignant than terrifying and they are intended to immortalise the nymphs. For the image of the hideous revenge meted out to the offspring of a god and a mortal, caused by unnatural interference, Machen went to the alchemists. Reynolds and Charlton point out (RC 46 1963) that Helen Vaughan's ending is a descent into primal matter, the 'tenebrae activae,' living darkness, that the alchemist Thomas Vaughan identified in his hermetic treatise, the *Lumen de Lumine*. We know that this work held a peculiar fascination for Machen, and he used the image again in other stories, 'The Novel of the White Powder' for example.

There were contemporary literary influences on this powerful final scene as well. We have already seen that Stevenson's *Dr Jekyll and Mr Hyde* must be counted a forebear of Machen's novel, and passages such as that in chapter ten of this story may well have remained in Machen's thoughts: '... the slime of the pit seemed to utter cries and voices ... the amorphous dust gesticulated and sinned ... that what was dead and had no shape should usurp the offices of life'. The air of scandal and corruption that surrounds Helen Vaughan may also have been suggested by Oscar Wilde's *The Picture of Dorian Gray*.

Machen told an American correspondent, Munson Havens, that he read Wilde's supernatural novel when it first appeared, in *Lippincott's Monthly Magazine*, July 1890 (published 20 June), and was 'a good deal impressed by it'. As *Pan* was begun in Summer 1890, during the period when Machen was meeting Wilde, it is quite likely that the influence of the latter's novel is to be seen in Machen's book.

In chapter twelve of Wilde's novel, the painter Basil Hallward reproaches Dorian with a long litany of infamies that have been associated with his name: 'They say that you corrupt every one with whom you become intimate, and that it is quite sufficient for you to enter a house, for shame of some kind to follow after'. Dorian, too, like Helen has been linked with the ruin, disgrace and suicide of young gentlemen. Helen is a female Dorian. Both are beauty concealing depravity, and evil.

The publisher John Lane was well qualified to take on a work with such a daring theme. In the year that *Pan* was published, he had issued the first three numbers of the *Yellow Book*, that touchstone of all that was most new and scandalous, with its provocative Beardsley drawings, and its writing on forbidden themes, such as Arthur Symons's poem 'Stella Maris', about a woman of the night. Its prospectus proclaimed 'while the *Yellow Book* will seek always to preserve a delicate, decorous, and reticent mien and conduct, it will at the same time have the courage of its modernness, and not tremble at the frown of Mrs Grundy,' but the critics were more exercised by the 'modernness' than by the modesty of the magazine, calling it

audacious, vulgar, hysterical, rowdy, lubricious, repulsive and in-
solent and demanding it be outlawed. Thus, Machen recalled in later
years that his book came out 'when Yellow Bookery was at its
yellowest' and 'profited by the noise' that the Decadent movement
was making, though he denied that his work itself derived from this
'ferment of the nineties'.

Nevertheless, it was not entirely out of keeping with the period.
Lane published it in his Keynotes series, named after the first title
by George Egerton (the pseudonym of Mary Chavelita Dunne,
1859-1945) a book of frank stories about women's loves and emotions, greeted with such adjectives as 'passionate,' 'wild,' 'animal,'
'throbbing,' 'dangerous', all of which might be applied to Helen
Vaughan. And Machen's novel, the fifth in the series, had resem-
blances to two other Keynotes already published. *The Dancing Faun*
by Florence Farr (later, like Machen, to be a member of the Order of
the Golden Dawn) made use of a similar pagan symbol and, although written with far more flippancy, it also has a female villain
who is not fully unmasked until the denouement. Machen's work
also has some kin with the book which immediately preceded his,
A Child of the Age by Francis Adams, a nineteen-year-old consump-
tive who in essence wrote his own story of 'a morbid, passionate
youth' and his desolate existence.

The book was originally entitled *Leicester: An Autobiographical
Novel* and it is curious that Machen used the name Francis Leicester
for the youth who dies into a pool of utter corruption in his later
'Novel of the White Powder'. Adams described Art as 'a misty
dream' with 'strange unnatural scents breathing from it; but under-
neath mud, filth, the abomination of desolation, the horror of sin and
death!' — again we see beauty regarded as a mask for foulness.

The response to *The Great God Pan* was almost as malodorous.
Machen shared with Beardsley, Max Beerbohm and others of the
Yellow Book school a perverse relish for the attacks of the critics, and
he was particularly fond of the epithets hurled at this novel. He
quoted them in an introduction to a 1916 reprint, again in his memoir
Things Near and Far (1923) and once more in a collection of reviews
of his work, *Precious Balms* (1924). Here are some of the best, or worst:
'The book is, on the whole, the most acutely and intentionally
disagreeable we have yet seen in English' (*Manchester Guardian*);
'This book is gruesome, ghastly, and dull ... the majority of readers
will turn from it in utter disgust' (*Lady's Pictorial*); '... It is not Mr

Machen's fault but his misfortune, that one shakes with laughter rather than with dread' (*Observer*); 'It is an incoherent nightmare of sex and the supposed horrible mysteries behind it, such as might conceivably possess a man who was given to a morbid brooding over these matters, but which would soon lead to insanity if unrestrained ...' (*Westminster*).

Despite the disapproval of the leader-writing and sermonising classes, the British reading public had long evinced a definite taste for strong terror: the demand for Gothic novels in the late eighteenth and early nineteenth century was well nigh insatiable, and during Machen's childhood the hero of many horror-seekers was Bulwer Lytton (Edward George, First Baron Lytton, 1803-1873), the statesman and investigator of the supernatural. His novels and stories are the foundation for much future work in the horror fiction field; in particular *A Strange Story* (1861) and *The Haunted and the Haunters: or The House and the Brain* (1859).

The reclusive Irish squire J. Sheridan Le Fanu (1814-1873) was another major contributor to the literature of the supernatural, with *Ghost Stories and Tales of Mystery* (1851), *The House by the Churchyard* (1863) and *In a Glass Darkly* (1872). *The Great God Pan* was thus firmly in a tradition of dark literature, much of which had also excited the distaste and reprobation of the reviewers; but like its predecessors this did not stop Machen's novel being eagerly received by a certain readership.

Nor was this merely the notoriety of a moment, for his novel was sufficiently well known to inspire at least two parodies, 'The Great Boo Plan and the Utmost Fright' by Arthur Compton Rickett (1895) and 'The Great Pan — demon' by Arthur A. Sykes, a *Punch* journalist, (1896) in both of which the 'mad doctor' theme is uppermost. This reflects the Jekyll and Hyde influence that most readers perceived, and this aspect was drawn upon by those, fewer, notices which praised *Pan*, as we have seen. Other comparisons were made though:

> Nothing so appalling as these tales has been given to publicity within our remembrance; in which, nevertheless, such ghastly fictions as Poe's 'Telltale Heart', Bulwer's *The House and the Brain*, and Le Fanu's *In a Glass Darkly* still are vividly present. The supernatural element is utilised with extraordinary power and effectiveness in both these blood-chilling masterpieces.
> (*Daily Telegraph*)

ARTHUR MACHEN

> The coarser terrors of Edgar Allen Poe do not leave behind them the shudder that one feels at the shadowed devil-mysteries of *The Great God Pan*.
> (*Liverpool Mercury*)

By comparison with some of the other authors on Lane's list, Machen was moderately successful. *The Great God Pan*'s boldness was admitted even by its detractors, some (admittedly provincial) press notices hailed him as a genius, and his name was now firmly in the public eye in a way it had never been for *Clemendy* or his translations. On the strength of this response, Machen could have carved for himself a career as a minor popular novelist, occasionally enjoying fashionable esteem. This was the route followed by others who were initially identified with the new and daring, such as H. de Vere Stacpoole, Robert Hichens or Edgar Jepson. To follow this course, he would have to compromise his quest for perfect expression in prose and his love of the courtly English of the seventeenth century, and tighten his plotting and structure. He did not do so.

The god Pan was to be frequently invoked in the fiction of the Edwardian period and just after, usually with a sense of youthful allurement and sometimes as a symbol for sexual freedom and license from the stifling moral climate that still clung from the previous century. In Saki's 'The Music on the Hill' (1911), E. M. Forster's 'The Story of a Panic' (1911) and Lord Dunsany's 'The Tomb of Pan' (1915) prigs pay the price for scorning the goatfoot boy. In Algernon Blackwood's 'The Man Who Played Upon the Leaf' (1910), and 'The Touch of Pan,' (1917) and, indirectly, in his collection *Pan's Garden* (1912), and novel *The Centaur* (1911), the god is a positive force, a wild exultation counterpoised to the stale artificiality of high society. The famous 'Piper at the Gates of Dawn' chapter in Kenneth Grahame's *The Wind in the Willows* (1908) strikes a fine balance between awe at the god's presence and adoration of his kinship. Pan in his more cosmic aspect is seen in E. F. Benson's story 'The Man Who Went Too Far' (1912) and his association with sexual avidity is seen in D. H. Lawrence's strange story 'The Last Laugh' (1928).

Pan's retinue of fauns, nymphs and satyrs dance too in the pages of these days, in Forster's 'The Curate's Friend' and 'The Road from Colonus,' (both in *The Celestial Omnibus*, 1911) implicitly in Huxley's *Antic Hay* (1923), to the extent that Max Beerbohm could say, with only a slight tinge of burlesque, 'current literature did not suffer from any lack of fauns ... We had not yet tired of them and their hoofs and their slanting eyes and their way of coming suddenly out of woods to wean quiet English villages from respectability' ('Hilary Maltby and Stephen Braxton,' 1917).

Such images as these were not in evidence before the playing with paganism that characterised the writings of the Decadents, and it is likely that Machen's novel, with its echoing title and its sinister Beardsley design, was influential in attaching to Pan a new mode, an association with the daring and dangerous. Such can scarcely have been his intention — although his early years do demonstrate a healthy interest in the erotic muse. But what had previously been a rustic, rather bucolic image, was now laced with images of illicit sex and cosmopolitan decadence.

Horror as a separate ghetto of literature had not yet been constructed when Machen's novel appeared, but it has since been almost irretrievably claimed for that genre, reprinted in anthologies such as *A Century of Horror Stories* edited by Dennis Wheatley (1934) and *Great Tales of Horror and the Supernatural*, edited by Herbert A. Wise and Phyllis Fraser (1944), a landmark American collection. Even modern critics are apt to purse their lips at the story: 'One is apt to be nauseated, not awestruck, by the picture of physical dissolution' (R & C 44 1963); the tale 'degenerates into a frenzied expression of horror over illicit sex' (SJ 21 1991). Its influence is to be found in a few specific places such as H. P. Lovecraft's 'The Thing on the Doorstep' and more recently M. John Harrison's *The Course of the Heart* (1992) but more generally as a precursor to all the 'Bride of Satan' type of films and thrillers.

Ultimately however *The Great God Pan* should be seen, despite Machen's protestations to the contrary, as a novel of the Decadence, of a piece with *Dorian Gray*, *The Dancing Faun*, with Kenneth Grahame's *Pagan Papers* (John Lane, 1893), with Beardsley's sly fauns and lascivious ladies.

In tracing the literary resonances of Machen's story we have left until last its original inspiration, 'a lonely house standing on the slope of a hill, under a great wood, above a river in the country where I was born,' which was 'just visible' from Machen's home, Llanddewi Rectory. The house was for the young Machen 'one of the many symbols of the world of wonder ... a great word in the secret language by which the mysteries were communicated' and,

33

on a journey with his father, it was 'more inexplicable, more wonderful, more significant, the nearer it was seen'. Stevenson, says Machen, understood that certain places demanded that a story should be written about them. And so it was that Bertholly, the white house on the hill above the gravely winding Usk, became the residence of Dr Raymond, the place where Pan was known by an innocent girl. (It is probably Bertholly, too, that sees the strange events of his 'Novel of the Black Seal' and 'The Bright Boy'.) It stands today, a hollow, forlorn ruin, riven with ivy and stripped of its whiteness, the victim of a great fire that ended its days as a fine house: and the curious pass it by as they follow the Usk Valley Walk and, knowing nothing of Machen's tales, could reasonably see it still as the scene of some sinister tragedy.

It was a house, too, that inspired the companion story to *The Great God Pan*. 'The Inmost Light' had its seed in the 'violent irruption of red brick in the midst of a green field' which Machen saw on one of his long walks from his digs in Clarendon Road, Notting Hill out to the suburbs of Harlesden. Machen was deeply affected by the intrusion of man's ugliest creations on nature, and his feelings may have a certain resonance for our more environmentalist times: 'the hedges are half ruined, half remaining ... the little winding brook is defiled ... one tree lies felled and withered. New, rabid streets are to rush up the sweet hillside, and capture it ... the well under the thorn is choked with a cartload of cheap bricks'. So horrified was Machen by the incursion of raw, red villas on what had been open country, that he imagined a horror, another sort of despoliation, equally callous and equally in the name of progress, into one of them. 'And so the man in my story, resting in green fields, looked up and saw a face that chilled his blood gazing at him from the back of one of those red houses ...' (TNF 119-21 1923) The scene is one of the most lingeringly memorable moments that Machen made.

Machen supplied 'The Inmost Light' at his publisher's request because *The Great God Pan* was not long enough to issue alone. The story, however, is not the makeweight this might suggest. While it has come too-close similarities to the novel, and relies equally heavily upon coincidence, it is more tightly drawn and as a consequence a better read. We meet Mr Dyson, a literary idler who reappears in other stories, always as a connoisseur of the curious, a sleuth of the singular. Dyson is a student of 'The science of the great city; the physiology of London; literally and metaphorically the greatest subject that the mind of man can conceive'. This possibly bombastic remark is offset ironically by Dyson's next comment, an epicurean aside — 'What an admirable salami this is' — for he is holding forth to a friend in a restaurant.

He continues, in a sentence that has often been cited to typify Machen's conviction that the strange and curious lie just around the corner:

> London is always a mystery ... You may point out a street, correctly enough, as the abode of washerwomen; but, in that second floor, a man may be studying Chaldee roots, and in the garret over the way a forgotten artist is dying by inches.

Dyson's rooms, affectionately described in the story, leave little doubt that he is allied to the current mode for the exotic and outré. We are to think of him as a jejune decadent, a follower of Beardsley, an aesthete:

> The floor glowed and flamed with all the colours of the East ... the lamplight, the twilight of London streets, was shut out with strangely worked curtains, glittering here and there with threads of gold ... the black and white of etchings not to be found in the Haymarket or in Bond Street, stood out against the splendour of a Japanese paper ... mingled fumes of incense and tobacco.

The story again concerns a doctor's unwise operation, this time on his wife. With his more stolid and sceptical friend Salisbury, Dyson uncovers two mysteries which prove to be intertwined: how and why Dr Black took the life of his wife in a way that perplexed experts; and the significance of a dazzling opal-like stone wrapped in a paper bearing a strange riddle. This nonsense rhyme proves to be a password by which Dyson tricks his way into possession of the splendid jewel, which once belonged to Dr Black. There is just a hint that some sinister conspiracy is connected to the stone, a hint that will take us ultimately to the world of Machen's next novel, *The Three Impostors*, with its arch-villain Dr Lipsius and his network of evil.

The conclusion of 'The Inmost Light,' Dr Black's notebook account of how he drew the soul from out of his wife and the vacuum was filled by a shameful and unutterable horror, is concise, controlled and has a macabre fascination. It is a little too vague to be convincing but still has considerable impact. The notion of conjuring the soul into some other receptacle may not have been original to Machen, but the abomination which replaces it in the victim's body is left mostly to the reader's imagination, an improvement on the final scene of *The Great God Pan*.

Machen wrote three more pieces involving the incorrigible Dyson, and in all three we are introduced to a new element in his stories: the Little People. These beings were created at a time when fairy folk were much in the air. W.B. Yeats's stories *The Celtic Twilight* had appeared in 1893 and in 1894 his drama *The Land of Heart's Desire*, about a young woman spirited away by the fairies, was produced. The Celtic fantasies of 'Fiona Macleod' (William Sharp) also began in this year, with the volume *Pharais*. And William Morris, whose *Earthly Paradise* Machen admired, published in 1894 *The Wood Beyond the World*, a fairy fantasy. But Machen's Little People are not the whimsical sprites of some fictions: they are dark, dwarfish and malevolent, the relics of a race, less than human, from primeval times: and Machen suggests they dwell among us still.

The first of these stories to appear was 'The Shining Pyramid', which was published in two parts in *The Unknown World*, May 1895. The magazine was edited by the occult scholar A. E. Waite, who had become a close friend of Machen's since their introduction to each other by Machen's wife in 1887. Waite was more deeply immersed in alchemical texts even than Machen, and had edited several key works for publication, as well as writing *The Real History of the Rosicrucians* (1887) and *Songs and Poems of Fairyland: An Anthology of English Fairy Poetry*. His magazine was intended to give space to 'all aspects of esoteric thought' (RAG 81-2 1987) and was mostly dedicated to non-fiction; Machen's story would have been among the livelier contributions.

Machen later called 'The Shining Pyramid' 'highly ingenious rubbish': he had written it 'purely for fun, to amuse myself' and although 'all good books are written for fun' it does not follow that he would claim much merit for it. It has been called 'a tepid rehashing' of another story, 'The Red Hand,' (SJ 23 1991) but it is not even clear which of these was written first.

Dyson is visited by an old friend, Vaughan, who lives in the West in a house 'with the ancient woods hanging all about it, and the wild, domed hills, and the ragged land'. A local girl has been lost in the hills and the people say she has been 'taken by the fairies'. At night, someone is delineating shapes using sharp flints on a path near Vaughan's house. The house has a similar site as Bertholly, 'on the lower slope of a great hill' above where 'a brook wound in and out in mystic esses'. An accretion of other curious circumstances passes before us: a chalk drawing, fires whose makers are unknown. The landscape itself seems steeped in horror; 'the fantastic limestone rocks hinted horror through the darkness'. The two men see in a hollow 'vague and restless forms' who speak like 'the hissing of snakes'; there are 'things like faces and human limbs' but it is as if they are 'some foul writhing growth'. A blaze of flame reveals them as like deformed children, 'almond eyes burning with evil and unspeakable lusts', flesh a ghastly yellow. This is a strong denouement which would certainly have excited disgust in the Victorian reader and has some power today. The living corruption it portrays has been seen before in *The Strange Case of Dr Jekyll and Mr Hyde*, *The Picture of Dorian Gray* and *The Great God Pan*.

The creatures are the prehistoric Turanian inhabitants of the country. What survives of them is not made clear, but they are supernatural rather than a lost tribe. Machen has pushed to its logical conclusion the ambivalent feelings for the Little People found in Celtic folklore, bringing to the fore the fear they inspire. His tale is ingenious, it is true, and his description 'rubbish' is certainly too hard a word for it, but it can only be regarded as a diversion.

Dyson makes his second appearance in Machen's episodic romance *The Three Impostors*, issued by John Lane as the eighteenth volume in the Keynotes series in November 1895. After finishing *The Great God Pan* in 1891, Machen had spent the next two years in the country, at Northend House, Turville, Buckinghamshire: he probably went there for the sake of his wife's health. Here he wrote two books, both he judged 'very bad', which he destroyed except for one episode which made its way into *The Three Impostors*, 'The Novel of the Dark Valley', an uninspired imitation of Conan Doyle's *The Valley of Fear*. These discarded books are the most substantial representation of a frequent self-censorship by Machen. His career is littered with cancelled chapters, abandoned fragments and visions which were never made flesh.

Machen and Amy returned to London in 1893 and again took rooms in Great Russell Street, close to the British Museum, and this was instrumental in prompting the theme of *The Three Impostors*. Although one of its most successful episodes takes place in Gwent, its main theme is the possibilities of sinister intrigue among the streets of London. Machen was later to evoke a scene by Dickens as 'a city translated into the very mystery of terror' and this is his theme in *Impostors*. Another Dickens commentator, Peter Conrad, has identified the same theme: 'In *A Tale of Two Cities* (1859) he nocturnally enchants an entire city, remarking that London by night is a celebration of dark secrets' (*Everyman History of English Literature*, 471, 1985).

If London gave the background to Machen's new work, there was a more direct inspiration too. The book was begun in spring 1894 and was being revised in early 1895: during this period public esteem for the dying Stevenson was at its height. 'It testifies,' Machen recorded of the book, 'to the vast respect I entertained for the fantastic *New Arabian Nights* manner of R.L. Stevenson', and, like Stevenson's work it is a series of linked episodes held together by the common thread of a great conspiracy. The four main parts are called 'novels': The Novels of the Dark Valley, Black Seal, Iron Maid and White Powder. We have seen the first and third of these already: the Iron Maid story had been one of Machen's earliest 'turnover' contributions and the Dark Valley episode was a leftover from unsuccessful work. These are the weakest two in the book, but the new 'novels' show Machen at his strongest in creating and sustaining dark horror: they are both often reprinted as separate stories.

In Stevenson's *New Arabian Nights* (1882), Prince Florizel of Bohemia, jaded by regal respectability, goes out to seek adventure in the London night, incognito and accompanied only by his aide, Colonel Geraldine. They stumble upon the Suicide Club, an ingenious but macabre society which combines a piquant form of euthanasia with a kind of murder by lot. The president of the club soon proves to have other villainous designs in progress or in prospect, and the reader comes to expect that each new and seemingly unconnected episode will eventually lead back to the Prince and his arch enemy. The insouciant style of the *New Arabian Nights*, even where it recounts violent death or other blackguardry, ensures we are always beguiled by the richly inventive fantasy. Stevenson repeated the formula and the frolic in a sequel of sorts, *The Dynamiter* (1885). A similar vein of wild gaiety and rococo embellishment may be found in other works which acknowledge a Stevenson influence: G.K. Chesterton's *The Man Who Was Thursday* (1908) and more especially *The Club of Queer Trades* (1905) and Michael Arlen's *These Charming People* (1923) and *Mayfair* (1925). In each of these, gentleman amateurs stalk strangeness in the labyrinthine streets of the world's capital, and face sinister conspiracies and devilish machinations. Machen's work, every inch the equal of the others for bizarrerie and bravado, has a darker tone, despite the banter between his two languid adventurers, the romantic, Dyson, and the realist, Phillips.

The Three Impostors has what the reader will later realise is an extremely chilling opening line, though it sounds quite harmless: '"And Mr Joseph Walters is going to stay the night?"'. As in both *The Great God Pan* and 'The Inmost Light', the focus for the story is a house which seems itself imbued with evil. It is rank and decaying: 'Broken urns lay upon the path, and a heavy mist seemed to rise from the unctuous clay; the neglected shrubberies, grown all tangled and unshapen, smelt dark and evil, and there was an atmosphere all about the deserted mansion that proposed thoughts of an opened grave'.

Machen's two idlers chance upon this ruin and remark upon how the sunset still glows in the grimy upper windows. It is only at the very end of the work, after many divagations, that the reader discovers a cruel and unknowing irony in their musing aestheticism.

This sardonic humour is also present in the very title of the book. The three impostors are, in the plot, lieutenants of Dr Lipsius, a Professor Moriarty figure whose crimes would require the attention of a grand inquisitor as much as that of a high court judge. They are impostors because they adopt disguises and characters in order to deceive Dyson and Phillips into revealing information about the whereabouts of a former confederate, the Young Man in Spectacles, who has made off with a gold Tiberius, a coin of priceless value, and also perhaps of talismanic significance for Dr. Lipsius's rites of evil. Yet 'The Three Impostors' was also the title of a medieval work of blasphemy and sin, probably mythical, which is said to have described Jesus and two other religious leaders as the three greatest charlatans the world has known. The sub-title of Machen's work, 'The Transmutations', has a double meaning too: it alludes not only to the disguises adopted by the impostors, but to the physical and other changes wrought upon characters in the stories the impostors tell.

The stories the impostors tell are untrue, not just in the sense that they appear in a work of fiction, but also in the scheme of the book itself. They are invented merely to entice the two dalliers in darkness into unwitting revelations of their investigations. This is a variation on the Stevensonian structure and it has caused some critics a difficulty: is there any point in striving for a sense of real evil and ancient credence in a supernatural tale, if the teller of the tale is from the outset undermined as a mere falsifier? As one critic put it, 'I confess I do not know what Machen is trying to get at in this undercutting his own work in this fashion. All I can fathom is that he is ridiculing the whole modern tendency of literary realism' (SJ 26 1990). This is the complaint of a critic not a general reader, for the reader does not know until late on in the book that the interposed narratives have no reality even in the book. At the time of reading, for the first time at any rate, they will be approached with as much suspension of disbelief as the rest of the work.

It would be unfair to unravel too much of *The Three Impostors* but it is worth giving particular attention to the two stories which have received most esteem. 'I do not think' said Machen 'that anybody before had written anything like the tales of "The Black Seal", or "The White Powder"' and he identified these two as 'I suppose the only things of much account in this volume [a reprint of *The Three Impostors*]... each of these tales is an experiment in the art of the wonder story, the story of events which are beyond the ordinary range of human observation, of events which we roughly call impossible'. 'The Novel of the Black Seal' was originally a werewolf tale but the transformation was, said Machen, 'unsatisfactory and unconvincing', and he destroyed this version. It is told to the rationalist Phillips by 'Miss Lally' the merciless confederate of Dr Lipsius, who is supposedly searching for her brother. The story she gives Phillips has some grounding in fact, for it concerns the ethnologist Professor Gregg, of whom her listener has heard, both for his academic work and his supposed accidental death the previous summer. Miss Lally, however, has a different explanation for his disappearance. She had been appointed governess to his two children, and accompanied the Professor to 'a country house in the west of England, not far from Caermaen, a quiet little town, once a city, and the headquarters of a Roman Legion. It is very dull there, but the countryside is very pretty, and the air is wholesome'. This description of Machen's homeland in the voice of a London academic is interesting for the author's assumptions about how the outside world might see his home; even so far as taking Monmouthshire as English not Welsh!

Professor Gregg has concluded that 'much of the folk-lore of the world is but an exaggerated account of events that really happened' and that accounts of disappearances, changelings, demons, and witches, may all have one source: remembrances of 'a race which had fallen out of the grand march of evolution' but retained 'certain powers which would be to us wholly miraculous'. The speech of this primitive species and some of their instincts would be close to that of the beasts. And there comes to him with a shock the thought that these creatures may not yet have gone: 'What if the obscure and horrible race of the hills still survived, still remained haunting wild places and barren hills, and now and then repeating the evil of Gothic legend?...'. Gregg possesses a Babylonian stone seal with indecipherable characters, and his researches uncover a comparable inscription 'Found on a limestone rock on the Grey Hills, Monmouthshire ... quite recent'. The seal holds the secret of human degeneration into primeval slime and animal form. Gregg has disappeared because he has gone out into the desolate Gwent hills to meet the Little People and test his theory; but, we are led to conjecture, they will not let him return.

Miss Lally's description of the house they have taken puts us in mind of the locality of Bertholly again:

> We were slowly mounting a carriage drive, and then there came to me the cool breath and the secret of the great wood that was above us; I seemed to wander in its deepest depths, and there was the sound of trickling water, the scent of the green leaves, and the breath of the summer night ... when I awoke and looked out of the bow window of the big, old fashioned bedroom, I saw under a grey sky a country that was still all mystery. The long, lovely valley, with the river winding in and out below, crossed in mid-vision by a medieval bridge of vaulted and buttressed stone ... and the woods that I had only seen in shadow the night before, seemed tinged with enchantment ...

Without ever bringing us directly into the presence of the sub-human species that his character has encountered, Machen creates an aura of menace and hideousness about them, in a masterpiece of macabre allusiveness. In doing so, we can have little doubt that he was tapping deep sources of unconscious dread for Victorians — the threat to their civilisation from an underclass of sordid, violent, secret, and subterranean terrorists, or from frighteningly alien races.

Novels in which anarchists or such perceived threats as 'the Yellow Peril' were a lurking conspiracy against order and respectability were beginning to be popular. It is not without significance that H.G. Wells' *The Time Machine*, with its disturbing picture of the underground, brute Morlocks, appeared in the same year as Machen's story (1895).

Whatever its origin may have been in the temper of the times, there is no doubt that Machen's tale does draw on authentic folk traditions showing that those taken by the fairies are seldom unmarked by their experience. In our times, the role of the Little People has perhaps been replaced by UFOs, with stories of 'alien abductions' following a similar sort of belief pattern. Machen would not have been bewildered by this further instance of pseudo-scientific explanation for what more ancient peoples would regard as the supernatural.

Machen's Little People have had a significant impact on the fantastic in fiction. H.P. Lovecraft, one of the most influential horror writers, with a horde of imitators, is best known for his stories of the 'Cthulhu Mythos', works in which a race of lurking Elder Gods and monstrosities from the deep are posited. The first tale in Lovecraft's loosely-connected saga, 'The Call of Cthulhu', is manifestly rooted in Machen's 'Novel of the Black Seal', even down to a professor who disappears after becoming obsessed by a cryptic bas-relief. Lovecraft (1890-1937) was a valetudinarian of limited private means, living in Providence, Rhode Island, who supplemented his income by ghostwriting, editing and journalism. He contributed around sixty highly-coloured stories to American 'pulp' magazines such as *Weird Tales* in the Twenties and Thirties, and also wrote a scholarly, wide ranging essay on *Supernatural Horror in Literature* (1927). Lovecraft discovered Machen's work in 1923 and quickly became an ardent enthusiast, praising him in his many vast letters to friends and working in references to Machen in several of his own stories. He is certainly the most significant American writer of dark fantasy since Poe, and today has several journals entirely devoted to his work and that of his disciples. Joshi, indeed, concludes 'I am convinced there is simply more to Lovecraft than to nearly any other weird writer, Poe perhaps not exempted' (SJ 228 1990). The idea of a malevolent atavistic survival and of the occult influence of landscape found in many of Lovecraft's stories must in some measure have been derived from Machen.

It is possible that Machen intended an additional twist to Miss Lally's tale which is not obvious to the reader at a glance. When we later learn that she is in league with the villainous Dr Lipsius, we must suppose that her yarn to Phillips was mere invention to mislead him. Yet elements of it at least are known by Phillips to be true, for there was a Professor Gregg, and he did disappear. So it is possible that he was in fact a victim of Dr Lipsius, disposed of perhaps for the sake of the rare black seal he owned, with its malevolent properties. Such, at least, is one of the turnings in the plot that could follow from the deceit and treachery of Miss Lally.

The plot of 'The Novel of the White Powder' is easily summarised: it is a sort of accidental Jekyll and Hyde. The hard-working, serious-minded law student, Francis Leicester, is prescribed a tonic which he has made up at an old apothecary's shop. It has the desired effect of giving him more zest for life but after a time it has a physical effect too, for he seems to be consumed by a black fire. Machen is making further use of the assumption he had pointed out to his publisher in connection with *The Great God Pan*: evil must have a scientific veneer to succeed with the audience of his day. Leicester's liquescent decomposition is grotesque and grand-guignol; the veil drawn over the fate of Professor Gregg is not used here, for we are brought straight to the presence of the lurid final scene. There is no doubt that this has an impact on the reader but it is perhaps not controlled quite well enough, and some have found something risible in the notion of the putrescent victim seeping through into the room below.

The exposition of Leicester's hideous fate, which follows the comparatively bald narrative, is of greater interest. The chemist asked to study the drug has also pursued an interest in metaphysics and his discovery of the true nature of the formula leads to a classic Machen expression of his convictions: 'The whole universe, my friend, is a tremendous sacrament; a mystic ineffable force and energy, veiled by an outward form of matter; and man, and the sun and the other stars, and the flower of the grass, and the crystal in the test-tube are each and every one as spiritual, as material, and subject to an inner working'.

The investigating chemist's theory is that the powders prescribed for Leicester had been overlong on the original chemist's shelf and had coincidentally undergone variations in temperature which replicated a process applied in medieval times to produce a devil's elixir, a dark sacrament: the wine of the Sabbath, which gave a piercing ecstasy to the participants in remote rites. Taken as a denouement in its own right, this is likely to make the reader gasp at the improbability (Machen himself called it 'wildly unlikely'), but we should recall that we are hearing a tall story told by one of Dr Lipsius's mocking disciples. It may even be that 'Helen' who narrates in the guise of the sister of Francis Leicester (it is Miss Lally again) is maliciously hinting at the tortures which await Lipsius's victim.

Removed from its context 'The White Powder' is unlikely to add force to Machen's reputation except for its sheer pungency; it is better regarded as integral to *The Three Impostors* where it emphasises the depravity of Helen's imagination. She is quite the most vindictive and insidiously cruel of the trio of villains, and it is perhaps regrettable that she does not reappear in Machen's stories with her 'shining hazel eyes', 'quaint and piquant' face and high laughter: Victorian fiction had need of such a vivid villainess.

But Machen was adamant that he had done with the Stevensonian romance, telling A.E. Waite 'I shall never give anybody a White Powder again'. There is an oblique suggestion in *Things Near And Far*, that there were those who so admired the work that they wanted more of the same, but for Machen this only produced irritation: 'I knew that all this was done and ended; that for me the vein was worked out and exhausted: utterly'.

Nevertheless, the novels of the Black Seal and the White Powder, often published separately from *The Three Impostors* in anthologies, have proved to be enduring classics in the field of weird fiction. E.F. Bleiler, probably the greatest authority in the field, described them as 'Beautifully narrated, highly imaginative, thought-provoking, even with a note of humour that is seldom noted. The mythology expressed in 'The Novel Of the Black Seal' ... has been very important historically' (EFB 333 1983).

Although stories of detection and fantastical adventure were still very much in favour with the public, it would appear *The Three Impostors* was received more in the shadow of *The Great God Pan* than in the light of the adventures of Sherlock Holmes, and its association with the provocative and bizarre may have led to its shunning in the wake of the trials of Oscar Wilde and the packhound pursuit of the aesthetes and decadents. Nevertheless, it attracted admiration from respectable literary figures. Jerome K. Jerome, in his autobiography, recalled lending a copy to Conan Doyle: 'Your pal Machen may be a genius all right; but I don't take him to bed with me again!' was the verdict. Later, poet laureate John Betjeman recalled: '*The Three Impostors* frightened me more than any book I read' (letter to Colin Summerford, 3 March 1943). Cyril Connolly said it was a great antidote to melancholy which 'gave great pleasure' because of 'a certain cheerful robustness in his portrait of evil' (*The Sunday Times* 20 October 1963). Machen was a constant proclaimer that the petty vices and vicious malfeasances of the everyday villain were beneath contempt: we should look for real evil, bold and barbarous, and Connolly has identified one of the attractions of the book, the thorough-going, fundamental nastiness of its villains. For Machen, one at least of the infamies perpetrated by his evildoers had an added personal relish: 'It gave me great pleasure, by the way, to murder, under singular circumstances of ingenious atrocity, a former employer of mine — see the chapter headed, "Strange Occurrence in Clerkenwell" ... this was Edward Walford'. The reference is to the mummification of an elderly antiquarian by Dr Lipsius's gang for the sake of the priceless treasure he owns. Machen wrote for *Walford's Antiquarian* journal in 1887, but presumably did not part amicably with the publisher.

The splendour of *The Three Impostors* is in its very improbability, its promise that adventure and fantastica lay just around the corner. In the gallant and insouciant manner in which they dally with danger, Dyson and Phillips belong with Sir Percy Blakeney (from Baroness Orczy's Scarlet Pimpernel novels) and with later characters like E.W. Hornung's Raffles and Dornford Yates's Berry. The riotous extravagance of the book is actually its strength not a weakness: it is what ensures it is still read and relished today, and re-read as often, when the more realistic and solemn novels of the time are thick and forgotten in booksellers' cheapest shelves. Machen gave a characteristically biting defence of his imaginative fantasies, as against the notion that 'The English Novel is only great when it is a sermon, a tract, or a pamphlet in disguise', in his preface to *The House of Souls* (1906), and it is surely all that needs to be said on the matter:

> He who carves gargoyles admirably is praised for his curious excellence in the invention and execution of these grinning monsters; and if he is blamed it is for bad carving, not because he failed to produce pet lambs.

Dyson and Phillips return in 'The Red Hand' (*Chapman's Magazine*,

December 1895). Machen may have considered that serial characters could gain the same public affection as Sherlock Holmes and Doctor Watson: his scholarly pair are more evenly matched than the immortal detective and his biographer, though neither comes alive as vividly as Holmes.

Its theme is that of the 'Novel of the Black Seal' in *The Three Impostors*. Dyson assures his sceptical counterpart 'The troglodyte and the lake-dweller, perhaps representative of yet darker races, may probably be lurking in our midst, rubbing shoulders with frock-coated and finely-draped humanity, ravening like wolves ... and boiling with the foul passions of the swamp and the black cave'. He says he will prove this in a single nocturnal walk. Instead, they stumble upon a murder, seemingly done with a prehistoric flint knife. A human hand is drawn in red chalk upon the wall nearby, caught in a grotesque gesture. An obscure note, apparently of astrological import and in an oriental style of writing, is found on the body. Dyson observes in a classic Machen phrase 'There are sacraments of evil as well as of good about us ... it is possible that man may sometimes return on the track of evolution, and it is my belief that an awful lore is not yet dead' and begins his resolute search for the 'black heaven' which proves to be a stone limned with spirals and labyrinths.

The story relies upon a chain of coincidences and some excessively inspired reasoning by Dyson, but Machen mischievously defuses these flaws by having Dyson proclaim a 'theory of improbability' which is more ingenious than convincing. The explanation of the killing of Sir Thomas Vivian and all its strange incidental details is akin to the resolution of a Holmes story, but Machen brings in an extra twist of primeval horror at the end. In the far west is a burial mound — Twyn Barlwm is intended — 'where those who live are a little higher than the beasts'. To a Victorian readership accustoming itself to the possibility of a descent from the apes, the reminder of more primitive antecedents still would have caused some revulsion. 'The Red Hand' is an enjoyable detective yarn with an undercurrent of horror, but is not prime Machen. By the end of 1895, he had pretty well finished with Mr Dyson's cases, so that we shall never know more of the affair of the yellow spectacles, alluded to in passing in 'The Shining Pyramid'. If Dyson's investigations always seem to rely on improbable leaps of the imagination, his reasoning is no more or less tenuous than that of Holmes. No one would claim him as an important character in literature, yet his adventures have a sinister insistence about them. We may feel that we too would like to find mystery and the bizarre at the street corner and in the deep countryside.

Three: Sorcery And Sanctity

From 1895 to 1902 Machen published no books, although he was a regular contributor to the journal *Literature* throughout 1898 and early 1899. This apparent inactivity, however, masks Machen's period of peak artistry, during which he wrote the novel called the most beautiful book in the world (by the American aesthete Carl Van Vechten in *Peter Whiffle*, Knopf, New York, 1922) and 'the most decadent book in all of English literature' (by the French critic Madeleine Cazamian in *L'Anti-Intellectualisme et L'Esthetisme*, Paris 1935). This was *The Hill of Dreams*. He also wrote the story acclaimed by many commentators as the greatest weird story ever written, 'The White People'; and those vignettes collected as *Ornaments In Jade*, which are certainly among the finest prose poems in the language.

In 1895 Machen and his wife moved from Great Russell Street to 4 Verulam Buildings, Gray's Inn, where he stayed until 1901. A neighbour was the fantasy novelist M.P. Shiel whose *Prince Zaleski* (1895) and *Shapes in the Fire* (1896) had also been published in the Keynotes series and who, like Machen, was writing his masterpiece. In Shiel's case this was *The Purple Cloud* (1901) in which a global disaster strikes down all but the narrator, who glories in his role as sole ruler of the world. The novel includes a tribute to his neighbour; a poet who died still writing, even though he must have thought there would be no one to see his work, is named Machen. Shiel recalled that on Sunday afternoons, 'quite a crowd of more or less literary people would fill Machen's drawing-room, filling it with smoke and sipping Benedictine which Machen presented with a certain unction and ceremony'. But, these gatherings aside, Shiel added, 'We lived in an island in the sea of London, rather touched with enchantment' ('The Good Machen', 22 June 1933).

Other frequent visitors to this informal salon included 'George Egerton', author of *Keynotes* and still regarded as a daring and dangerous young woman; James Welch, the comic actor and champion of Shaw's plays; Edgar Jepson, popular author and man about town; Olivia Shakespear, confidante of Yeats and author of *Beauty's Hour: A Phantasy* (in *The Savoy*, the journal edited by Arthur Symons and illustrated by Beardsley); and Jerome K. Jerome.

The Machen who recalled of the 1880s 'I knew very few people at all in the whole of London, and none of them intimately or very cordially: I certainly knew no one of like interests to my own' (AFL, 19 1993) had over a period of several years found a circle of like minds, and from this time on he was never to be without a similar group of friends. Forty years later, Machen recalled attending a 'Keynotes Dinner' given by the publisher John Lane in 1895, and meeting Max Beerbohm fleetingly, 'at Theodore Wratislaw's' in 1899. Wratislaw, descended from a Bohemian Count, was a minor poet of the nineties, whose delicate, wistful verses were assembled as *Caprices* (1893). He also contributed to *The Savoy*, but wrote virtually nothing from 1900 to his death in 1933. These two stray recollections, preserved by chance in the letters of Machen's old age, suggest that his acquaintance with the literati of the nineties was greater than he usually allowed himself to say, either because of modesty, or a sense that his association with the fin de siècle mode was a diversion from the real essence of his work. He told a correspondent in 1945, 'I was remarkable for hardly knowing any of the nineties men at all' (SL 202 1988) and specifically includes poets Ernest Dowson and Arthur Symons in this: elsewhere he recorded that he never met Beardsley, the illustrator of his two Keynotes books.

Machen began what was to become his masterpiece, *The Hill of Dreams*, shortly after the publication of *The Three Impostors,* in autumn 1895. It was a conscious attempt to break away from the Stevensonian style of the previous book. 'With some assistance from reviewers', Machen noted, 'it was borne in on me that I must smash this borrowed manner to bits and build up another manner, which should be more worthy of being called a style, an expression of individuality.' This work was painfully difficult for him: 'now, I found, I was halting, uncertain, harsh, tautological' and his detailed descriptions years later of the mental anguish he endured before completing the book bear witness to the seriousness with which he regarded the craft of writing.

The Hill of Dreams is a short novel in seven chapters, four set in a fictionalised Caerleon (Caermaen) and its surrounding country, and three in a dreary West London quarter. It tells of a boy's quest for beauty through literature and dreaming, and finally and tragically through a nameless drug. The numinous sensuality of the visions he experiences by a kind of spiritual alchemy are contrasted with the poverty, loneliness and hardship he suffers for the sake of his visions. The pettiness and spite of the small-town citizens of Caermaen, and the squalor of the London streets, are bitingly portrayed, but against this satirical realism, we also witness the boy's transformation of actual scenes into imaginary realms: the decayed Roman city becomes a garden of marble and fountains and ilex, the London slums flame into a mad orgy. Ultimately, the novel's theme is the descent from an ideal of spiritual beauty to a fevered nightmare of depravity.

Machen had read a description of Sterne's *Tristram Shandy* as 'a picaresque of the soul' and was moved to attempt what he called 'a "Robinson Crusoe" of the soul,' in which the loneliness would not be that of a man on a desert island but of one who suffers 'mental isolation, because there is a great gulf fixed spiritually between him and all whom he encounters'. But to this starting-point were added 'the thoughts of the country in which I was born and bred, which counts for a great deal' and 'the pains of literature, semi-starvation and loneliness which I had actually experienced'. That the book is semi-autobiographical will be clear to any reader. The torment and frustration of the youthful protagonist, Lucian Taylor, at the crassness and innate cruelty of the worldly when faced with the truly artistic or idealistic is conveyed so feelingly that we cannot doubt the closeness to Machen's own experiences. Richard Ellmann has called Wilde's Dorian Gray 'aestheticism's first martyr': Lucian Taylor is in the same martyrology. It is as if Walter Pater's pagan saint, Marius the Epicurean, in the classical romance of that title (1885), had been brutally transported to the penury and meanness of Gissing's *New Grub Street* (1891). Machen recalled in 1925 that he had 'long venerated Pater by rumour' until he actually read him, when he found his prose dull. Nevertheless, he conceded that Pater's aesthetical standpoint 'had the root of the matter' in its understanding of the relationship of art and the spirit (AFL 32 1993).

The 'decadence' in the book derives partly from certain scenes that would not be out of place in a work of Baudelaire or Huysmans or Swinburne, but more especially from the finely-wrought prose style

Machen had perfected. Lord Alfred Douglas, in his review of the
novel, used his own mannered but exquisitely modulated prose
style to convey Machen's: 'his prose has the rhythmic beat of some
dreadful Oriental instrument, insistent, monotonous, haunting; and
still the soft tone of one careful flute sounds on, and keeps the nerves
alive to the slow and growing pain of the rhythmic beat ... It is like
some dreadful liturgy of self-inflicted pain, set to measured music:
and the cadence of that music becomes intolerable by its suave
phrasing and perfect modulation. The last long chapter with its
recurring themes is a masterpiece of prose, and in its way unique'.

A.G. Stock has pointed out (AGS 39-40 1961) that 'A poet's characteristic rhythms are an expression of the frame of mind in which
poetry comes to him'. What is true of poetry can be true also of
Machen's heightened prose; what does its rhythm tell us? It says
something, I think, about his debt to Swinburne. 'I began to write
because I bought a copy of Swinburne's *Songs Before Sunrise*' Machen
states in *Far Off Things*:

> ... certainly that volume of *Songs Before Sunrise* was to me quite
> cataclysmic. First there was the literary manner of the book,
> which to me was wholly strange and new and wonderful, and
> then there was the tremendous boldness of it all, the denial of
> everything that I had been brought up to believe most sure
> and sacred; the book was positively strewn with the frag-
> ments of shattered altars and the torn limbs of kings and
> priests.

The immediate impact of Swinburne was only to make Machen
write much derivative verse, of which *Eleusinia* is the only survivor.
But the lingering influence on Machen is still to be seen in the prose
style of *The Hill of Dreams*. 'Swinburne's rhythm is hypnotic, drown-
ing thought in a monotonous tide of feeling generated by the sound
of words' comments Professor Stock: the parallel with Douglas's
evocation of Machen's prose is striking. And Lucian Taylor's own
literary credo has the same keynote:

> Language, he understood, was chiefly important for the
> beauty of its sounds, by its possession of words resonant,
> glorious to the ear, by its capacity, when exquisitely arranged,
> of suggesting wonderful and indefinable impressions, per-
> haps more ravishing and further removed from the domain
> of strict thought than the impressions excited by music itself.

ARTHUR MACHEN

Here lay hidden the secret of suggestion, the art of causing sensation by the use of words.

Again, the emphasis on the sound of words, the appeal beyond rationality ('strict thought'). This view of literature as a kind of spellmaking or magical incantation, influencing the reader by the subtle deployment of charged and chantlike words, links Machen with the Symbolist poets of France and Belgium and with their paler English Decadent votaries. For Mallarmé, arch-apostle of the Symbolists, the 'one true kind' of literary life 'consists in awakening inner harmonies and meanings' while W.B. Yeats, in *The Symbolism of Poetry* (1900) propounded: 'All sounds, all colours, all forms ... evoke indefinite and yet precise emotions or, as I prefer to think, call down among us certain disembodied powers, whose footsteps over our heart we call emotions ... poets and painters and musicians ... are continually making and unmaking mankind'. In certain passages in *The Hill of Dreams*, indeed in virtually the whole of the fourth, or Roman, chapter, in which Lucian immerses himself in a sensuous contemplation of an imagined ancient Latin world, with tavern, temple, garden, villa and amphitheatre burningly vivid, all plot and incident are secondary, and significant only in the sense that the trellis is necessary for the vine, providing the framework for sinuous, lingering sentences and intoxicating phrases. It is this prose poetry that distinguishes the book most of all from its contemporaries, giving it a potency and imperishability that most of the serious and acclaimed novels of the day, dealing also with the theme of the individual's spiritual pilgrimage, do not have: the earnest and 'improving' tone of Mrs Humphrey Ward's *Robert Elsmere* (1888) or J.H. Shorthouse's *John Inglesant* (1881) did not long survive the new century.

Yet there is a decadence of incident not only of technique or intention. This is established in the first chapter, in the scene that gives the book its title. On a day of blazing 'Provencal' heat Lucian walks to an old Roman fort, with overgrown ramparts, a ring of oak trees, a dense thicket of rank growth with oozing mud and sickly fungus — all pungently described — and, finally, a clearing of 'sweet close turf', of 'clean firm earth from which no shameful growth sprouted' where he 'lay down at full length on the soft grass', with the knowledge that 'he was utterly alone'. Stripping, 'he lay in the sunlight, beautiful with his olive skin, dark haired, dark eyed, the

52

gleaming bodily vision of a strayed faun'. Staring at the simulacra of the knotted and twining boughs in the thicket, he seems to see a stirring — 'the wood was alive'. Sleep comes, and when he awakes he is shocked to find his nudity, and to recall a vision — a dream or otherwise? — of a figure kissing him as he lay.

It is not hard to find the incident a metaphor of sexual awakening, and much of the imagery was clearly written with this intention. But the passage is also significant as an inversion, consciously or not, of the key section of Richard Jefferies' *The Story of My Heart* (1883) with which Machen was familiar. In this spiritual autobiography, a classic of its kind, Jefferies describes his visits to an embanked hillfort, with its 'sweet short turf' where he was 'utterly alone' and where he lies down on the grass and experiences, or rather induces, 'an emotion of the soul beyond definition' inspired by a heightened form of pantheism. 'the inexpressible beauty of all filled me with a rapture, an ecstasy, an inflatus ... it was a passion. I hid my face in the grass, I was wholly prostrated, I lost myself in the wrestle, I was rapt and carried away'.

Jefferies described an actual place, Liddington Hill in Wiltshire: it is highly significant that Machen did not. Though a familiar of the ancient places of Gwent, he invented the hill of dreams, telling John Gawsworth years later that it was imagined to be near a place called Common Cefn Llwyn. The invention was, it is reasonable to assume, influenced by the memory of Jefferies' hill shrine. But whereas Jefferies dated the beginnings of his spiritual awakening — the 'Story of My Heart' of the title — from his experiences on the hill, for Lucian it is the origin of his spiritual descent, for he is convinced 'he had sinned against the earth, and the earth trembled and shook for vengeance'.

Originally entitled *Phantasmagoria*, Machen called his novel *The Garden of Avallaunius* when it was first published, in periodical form, in 1904: but opted for the title it now bears because of fears that 'Avallaunius' — a personal name meaning 'man of Avalon' — would be mispronounced. But changing titles change too the focus of the book. 'Phantasmagoria' seems to draw us closer to the frenzied, kaleidoscopic sequence of images towards the end of the book, where Lucian's visions are out of control. But the word is used in the first chapter when Lucian, wakening in his bed the day after the visit to the hillfort, is seized at first by the same panic, but 'in the plain room it seemed all delirium, a phantasmagoria'. The dictionary definition for phantasmagoria — 'shifting scene of real or imagined figures' helps us to see that Machen may have intended in the original title a deliberate ambiguity both about what happens on the hill, and as to the actuality of all Lucian's later visions. The second title, the 'Garden', puts the emphasis on the fourth chapter, since Avallaunius is Lucian's alter ego in his reveries of the Roman town. Lucian is convinced he has found the solution to the Hermetic Mystery, the alchemists' supposed striving to turn base metal into gold: it is an allegory of the transformation of the coarseness of day to day life into the beautiful essence of aesthetic thought:

> 'Only in the court of Avallaunius is the true science of the exquisite to be found.'
> He saw the true gold into which the beggarly matter of existence may be transmuted by spagyric art; a succession of delicious moments, all the rare flavours of life concentrated, purged of their lees, and preserved in a beautiful vessel. The moonlight fell green on the fountain and on the curious pavements, and in the long sweet silence of the night he lay still and felt that thought itself was an acute pleasure, to be expressed perhaps in terms of odour or colour by the true artist.

The final title, though, brings us back to his first experience, and its significance for the rest of the book. In what way is the old Roman fort a hill of dreams? Is it a place of magic itself, was Lucian visited by some supernatural figure or by the lovely country girl Annie, whom he afterwards worships from afar? Was he bewitched there, does all else follow inexorably, a 'doom' upon him? Did he in fact sin against the earth?

It is part of the allure of the book that Machen does not give us outright answers to these questions, and denies us any plain demarcation between the external and internal elements of Lucian's life. But the climax of the book, the sixth and seventh chapters in a London that recalls James Thomson's *City of Dreadful Night* (1874), a carnival of grinning spectres, is suggestive. We may put everything down to madness or to drugged hallucinations, yet there remains an occult implication.

Armed, as Machen had been, with a modest legacy, Lucian takes lodgings in an impoverished region of London and works night and day at perfecting his literary art. Newly confident, he sees his adventure on the hill as 'boyish imagination. There was no terror nor amazement now in the green bulwarks, and the stunted under-growth did not seem in any way extraordinary'. But isolation, hunger and the constant frustration of his aims in literature, 'searching for hieroglyphic sentences, for words mystical, symbolic' begin to take their toll, and he returns to his old fears:

> He had thought when he closed his ears to the wood whisper and changed the fauns' singing for the murmur of the streets ... that he had put off his old life, and had turned his soul to healthy activities, but the truth was that he had merely exchanged one drug for another. He could not be human, and he wondered whether there were some drop of fairy blood in his body that made him foreign and a stranger in the world.

His dark speculations become increasingly obsessive, but Machen does not spell out whether we are witnessing the working of some malediction upon him, or the wanderings of a hypersensitive mind weakened by privation and loneliness. Lucian comes to believe, by turns, 'that he himself still slept within the matted thicket, imprisoned by the green bastions of the Roman fort'; that he was 'in communion with evil', that drunken revellers spilling from a London pub recognise him as a fellow celebrant of a Bacchic orgy; and that a bronze-haired street courtesan who offers to 'go for a walk' with him is destined to be his partner in evil. The tumult of delirious images quickens as the book's conclusion nears, and Machen later revealed that he wrote the seventh and last chapter in a sudden surge of inspiration which suggests the stream-of-consciousness techniques later adopted by the avant-garde. Remembering again the incident on the hill, 'it seemed as if a woman's face watched him from between the matted boughs, and that she summoned to her side awful companions who had never grown old through all the ages': finally, in a vision of frenzy and flame, he sees himself perform the 'marriage of the sabbath' with the bronze-haired woman, within the circle of the hill.

For all its rich language, Machen exercises considerable authorial restraint in *The Hill of Dreams*, leaving the reader to decide whether the book belongs with De Quincey's *Confessions of an English Opium Eater*, as a record of drugged visions; with Wilde's *The Picture of Dorian Gray*, as a Faustian fable delineating the penalty for solipsistic aestheticism; with Poe's *The Fall of the House of Usher*, since in the final segment Lucian's fate becomes entwined with a mouldering, derelict house he has found; or with *The Great God Pan* as a further revelation of the activities of the immortal creatures Lucian thinks he glimpsed in the undergrowth of the old fort; these among many other possible interpretations.

The Hill of Dreams has been seen as 'an epilogue to English decadence, in which beauty and death are represented as inextricably fused' (LT 267 1980) — the theme too of *The Great God Pan*. There is no doubt that Lucian Taylor's obsession with literary style, with the contemplation of the exquisite, with the investigation of the strange (in Chapter four he 'makes a singular study of corruption' — physical and moral), and his retreat from the mass of humanity, and broodings upon pagan shapes, are all characteristics of the Decadence.

Machen always maintained that, despite his association with Wilde, and other relevant figures of the period, he was not truly part of the nineties ambience. Yet *The Hill of Dreams* suggests he may have been influenced by the prevailing modes, and moods, of the period more than he knew, or was prepared to admit, and it is significant that his major fiction in the new century, *A Fragment of Life* and *The Secret Glory*, while retaining an allegiance to exalted spiritual and aesthetic precepts, banishes the darker visions from the canvas, dwelling solely upon the supernal. It is as if Machen was turning his back on any further evocation of images of evil, in the manner of Huysmans or Beardsley making their peace with the Catholic Church at the last. 'The Hill of Dreams, as you say justly, is not autobiography, since I am still alive,' Machen wrote to Vincent Starrett in 1917. But many of the English decadents such as Dowson, Johnson, Wilde, Beardsley, Crackanthorpe and Davidson, had died in circumstances not entirely remote from those of Lucian's death, and in writing *The Hill of Dreams* Machen may in part have been working through a vision of what might have been, for him too. The publisher Grant Richards rejected *The Hill of Dreams* when Machen offered it to him in Spring 1897, and in his reply Machen noted: 'You object to the environment of the beginning; but it is the environment which largely shapes the character: it is these *bacilli* of the village which are largely responsible for the pathological condition of the patient'. Besides suggesting Machen's own understanding of the book, as a record of mental and physical deterioration, we are reminded that the book's roots are in Caerleon, and whatever infected Lucian had the potential to blight Machen's life too. It is because *The Hill of Dreams* is a study in potential autobiography that it is written with such searing, morbid compulsion, and the reader is both fascinated and appalled.

Richards was not the only publisher to reject the book. Methuen, John Lane, the Unicorn Press and others all advised Machen, as he afterwards recalled, not to publish the book because 'it was so poor and weak and dull'. And so, remarkably enough, it first appeared in *Horlicks' Magazine,* edited for the proprietor of the malted milk drink company by Machen's friend A.E. Waite: it was serialised here from July to December 1904, and what the readers made of it would be well worth knowing. Grant Richards finally changed his mind and published it in book form in 1907, ten years after he had rejected it.

But this long wait for recognition for what Machen always regarded as his finest work, was as nothing compared with the time between his composition of ten prose poems, some originally fragments from *The Hill of Dreams*, in 1897, and their first appearance as a collection twenty-seven years later. It is a measure of the Anglo-Saxon distaste for the prose poem as a form, as well as of the specific difficulty Machen had in finding publishers, that even after this interval the *Ornaments in Jade*, as they were entitled, were issued in a limited edition of one thousand only.

Each of these prose pieces recounts a single incident in which there is an encounter with the celestial or satanic. A dejected, disillusioned man sees the commonplace world transformed around him, so that in 'The Holy Things' the harsh sights, sounds and smells of a Holborn street seem like elements of a beautiful liturgy. In 'Psychology', a mild recluse meditates upon the wild desires which lurk inside us all, and carefully records 'all the secret thoughts of the day, the crazy lusts, the senseless furies, the foul monsters that his heart had borne, the maniac phantasies that he had harboured': we are reminded of Yeats's phrase '... the dark folk who live in souls/of passionate men, like bats in the dead trees' (from 'To Some I Have Talked with by the Fire', 1899), and of course of *Jekyll and Hyde* once again. In 'The Turanians', a girl encounters a band of gypsies, descendants of that primeval race Machen had linked in earlier stories to the 'Little People': she revolts against her tame home life to taste of their pagan ways. Similarly in 'The Ceremony', a woman is haunted by the remembrance of some secret worship at a stone idol in her childhood, and overcomes her modesty to re-enact there 'the antique immemorial rite'. 'The Rose Garden', the most ethereal of the pieces, depicts a woman attaining a rare communion of soul as she looks out over a rose garden during the deep tranquillity of night.

What cannot be conveyed in any summary of these pieces, or of the other five in the collection, is Machen's vivid evocation of the high splendours and the shaded secrets of the spiritual world, which he here distills into sentence after sentence that has the harmony of the psalms and yet the voluptuousness of the most vice-steeped verses of the decadents. It is as if he has perfected the quest for the elusive, suggestive prose that Lucian Taylor pursues in *The Hill of Dreams*: 'that desire of a prose which should sound faintly, not so much with an audible music, but with the memory and echo of it'; as if he has realised Lucian's ambition 'To win the secret of words, to make a phrase that would murmur of summer and the bee, to summon the wind into a sentence, to conjure the odour of the night into the surge and fall and harmony of a line'.

The prose poem was the quintessential form of expression for the French Symbolists. Baudelaire, Mallarmé and Huysmans all devoted some of their craft to it, alongside their better-known work, while for some lesser figures, such as Ephraim Mikhael and Saint-Pol-Roux, it was the preferred medium. An influential anthology of translations from the French by the American poet Stuart Merrill, *Pastels in Prose*, appeared in 1890. William Dean Howells (1837-1920), the American novelist and critic, in his introduction to this book, describes the prose poem as 'a peculiarly modern invention' and looks to Turgenev as the first great proponent of the form. Without proposing a specific definition, he notes that the French examples in the volume have in common a 'beautiful reticence', adding 'The very life of the form is its aerial delicacy, its soul is that perfume of thought, of emotion, which these masters here have never suffered to become an argument. Its wonderful refinement, which is almost fragility, is happily expressed in the notion of "Pastels"' (PIP vii-viii 1890). Raymond Bantock, in the first international anthology of the form, notes that the prose poem has in common with the verse poem, 'beautiful ideas, a lyrical inspiration, singleness of purpose, completeness of conception, metaphor, simile, alliteration, the intoxication of words' but that it benefits from the absence of 'the artificial aids of rhyme and metre', adding that instead 'we are face to face with the "kernel" or inner meaning, with the essence of the poem itself in its most undiluted form' (RB xviii 1925). Bantock quotes Baudelaire, with Turgenev the other great progenitor of the form as aspiring to 'the miracle of poetical, musical prose, without rhythm, without rhyme, supple enough and apt enough to adapt itself to the movements of the soul, to the swaying of a dream, to the sudden throbs of conscience' (RB 28-9).

There is no doubt that Machen was a successful craftsman in this medium, but in Britain the form never won a devoted following and even those working in a similar fashion tended to use a different term: 'Fiona Macleod' (William Sharp) called his pieces 'prose rhythms', Richard Le Gallienne's brief, whimsical essays were entitled *Prose Fancies* (1894) and the realist short story writer Hubert Crackanthorpe's one foray in this field used the description *Vignettes* (1896). Machen seems always to have been abreast of contemporary literary developments, and so would probably have been aware of most of these attempts in the sphere of the brief prose sketch, but his own work, which he refers to only as 'a short collection of experiments' does not bear any signs of their influence. We may perhaps see them as belonging with those collections of short fantasies written in heightened prose which seem to cluster at the end of the century: Shiel's *Shapes in the Fire* (1896), Yeats' *The Secret Rose* (1897), R. Murray Gilchrist's *The Stone Dragon* (1894) and J.H. Pearce's *Tales of the Masque* (1894). As neither the British reading public nor publishers viewed his efforts in the conventional novel format with any sympathy, so Machen must have known even as he made them that these prose pieces would not quickly get a hearing.

The brevity of the pieces results in another quality which places them in a wider literary context: elusiveness. Roger Dobson has noted (*Machenalia* volume II, 1990) that the pieces 'may be viewed almost as a collaboration between author and reader. Because these tales represent Machen at his most enigmatic ... we must decipher much of the coded significance of the narratives, and read between the lines of the text ... Decades before it became fashionable for writers such as Jorge-Luis Borges, Alain Robbe-Grillet and John Fowles to do so, Machen is playing fictional games with the reader'. Machen's reticence in several instances leaves the reader to decide on the significance of key images: he is practising again the art of 'suggesting wonderful and indefinable impressions' advocated in *The Hill of Dreams*.

'The Turanians', 'The Ceremony', 'Midsummer' and 'Witchcraft' all show young women drawn to the secret and alluring rites of paganism in one form or another, and this was to provide the theme of Machen's most successful weird story, 'The White People', written in 1899 as part of a more ambitious work which failed to emerge.

The story has a prologue and epilogue which are mostly dialogue between a mystic recluse, Ambrose, and a more sceptical visitor, Cotgrave: the characters are essentially a reprise of the Dyson/Phillips roles in *The Three Impostors*. Its opening words, spoken by Ambrose, are a memorable summary of Machen's beliefs: 'Sorcery and sanctity ... these are the only realities. Each is an ecstasy, a withdrawal from the common life'. Ambrose goes on to distinguish between the mundaneness of ordinary crime, and real spiritual evil, 'a passion of the solitary, individual soul', which offends against the very nature of things, the universal order. 'What is sin?' asks Cotgrave, and Ambrose replies in a passage which is often quoted by connoisseurs of cosmic and visionary horror:

> What would your feelings be, seriously, if your cat or your dog began to talk to you, and to dispute with you in human accents? You would be overwhelmed with horror. I am sure of it. And if the roses in your garden sang a weird song, you would go mad. And suppose the stones in the road began to swell and grow before your eyes, and if the pebble that you noticed at night had shot out stony blossoms in the morning?

Ambrose elaborates on the true nature of sin by use of biblical terminology. Holiness is 'an effort to recover the ecstasy and knowledge that was before the Fall. But sin is an effort to gain the ecstasy and the knowledge that pertain alone to angels, and in making this effort man becomes a demon'. To convince Cotgrave further, Ambrose lends him a notebook, 'one of the choicer pieces in my collection', bound in green morocco, with fine paper, gilt decorations and a delicate odour of age about it: we note the aestheticism of the book's description.

There follows a long extract from 'The Green Book' which is amongst the most extraordinary writing Machen achieved. The manuscript is the diary of an adolescent girl, perhaps about fifteen years old, and Machen's replication of child-like directness and honesty is utterly convincing and sustained for thirty pages, mostly solid blocks of unparagraphed text, without any real flaw in tone. All of the languor and luxurance of the style he had woven for *The*

Hill of Dreams and the prose poems has been stripped away and we
have a great torrent of simple language such as might be expected
from an excited child telling of her adventures: with the crucial
difference, chillingly effective, that some of the words — 'Aklo',
'Chian', 'Voor', 'Dols', 'Jeelo' have no meaning, or no ordinary
meaning, and the reader soon realises that their significance can only
be sinister.

For the girl has been led, unknowingly, by her nurse into the ways
of 'the most secret secrets' of the Old Faith: she has learned forbidden
languages, strange dances, an enactment she calls the Comedy, and
three ceremonies, White, Green and Scarlet. For her, all of the landscape around her home is living, the stones and the trees and the
springs seem to have inner emotions which affect her own:

> I went on into the dreadful rocks. There were hundreds and
> hundreds of them. Some were like horrid-grinning men; I
> could see their faces as if they would jump at me out of the
> stone, and catch hold of me, and drag me with them back into
> the rock, so that I should always be there. And there were
> other rocks that were like animals, creeping, horrible, ani-
> mals, putting out their tongues, and others were like words
> that I could not say, and others like dead people lying on the
> grass. I went on among them, though they frightened me, and
> my heart was full of wicked songs that they put into it: and I
> wanted to make faces and twist myself about in the way they
> did ....

Machen blends into the girl's narrative her retelling of stories told
to her by her nurse, who heard them from her great-grandmother.
These 'odds and ends of folklore' as Machen called them, are versions of authentic traditional tales about otherworldly maidens
whose beauty entraps mortal men in fairyland, or who are themselves seized by dark and ominous strangers, and they suggest,
without making explicit, where the girl's involvement in her nurse's
'games' with clay effigies will lead, especially when she begins to try
experiments of her own and to find white companions who appear
when she needs them.

The naivety of the girl's account, half-innocent, half-complicit, like
children who have a secret society with its own hideouts, passwords,
rules and purposes, all hidden from adults, is what gives 'The White
People' its awful power, as if the reader is witnessing at first hand

the deadly stalking of a child victim, powerless to intervene. Machen achieves the supreme fictional success of removing any sense of authorial involvement: as T.E.D. Klein has observed, '"The Green Book" seems an authentic artefact, the actual product of an encounter with primeval forces, not merely a description of them' (PEHS 277 1986).

The denouement is explained by Ambrose when Cotgrave returns the book to him: the girl was found lying by a Roman crafted stone, concealed in a thicket; '"She had poisoned herself — in time"'. Machen does not spell out what fate she avoided, but we are reminded of the Roman pillar quoted at the conclusion of *The Great God Pan*, dedicated to Nodens, 'god of the Great Deep or Abyss ... on account of the marriage ... beneath the shade'. We may reasonably infer that the girl of the Green Book saved herself from the fate of Helen Vaughan and her mother, handmaidens of Pan.

The allusiveness and the conviction of Machen's writing are part of the strength of 'The White People'. But the story's force also derives from its range: here is no isolated episode of a haunting or a strange incident, the staple diet of supernatural stories, but a landscape in which all things have a sinister and hidden meaning beyond their outward appearance, in which a word or a thought or gesture will transform tree, stone, mound into sentient beings, like the dog or the rose or the stone of Ambrose's dictum about the essence of evil. We cannot walk anywhere, the evidence of 'The Green Book' tells us, without the knowledge that a lurking presence waits to fulfil its potential. It is this characteristic of the story that led H.P. Lovecraft to praise its 'almost unlimited power in the intimation of potent hideousness and cosmic aberration' (*Supernatural Horror in Literature*, 1927).

Machen acknowledged that the story 'contains some of the most curious work that I have ever done, or ever will do. It goes, if I may say so, into very strange psychological regions,' but the verdict of recent critics has been even more enthusiastic, typified by E.F. Bleiler: 'This document ('The Green Book') is probably the finest single supernatural story of the century, perhaps in the literature' (EFB 334 1983): and by T.E.D. Klein, whose novel *The Ceremonies* (1985) was inspired by the story; 'It remains the purest and most powerful expression of ... the "transcendental" or "visionary" supernatural tradition ...' (PEHS 277 1986).

Apart from some very late stories written in response to commercial pressure, this was the last story Machen wrote in which horror is the dominant theme. The philosophical Ambrose seems to return in the guise of 'the Hermit' in Machen's next book, *Hieroglyphics*: and his later fiction all aspires to convey sanctity, not sorcery.

Four: Mysteries and Visions

In early 1899 Machen finished in very short order a book which probably emerged from his work on the journal *Literature*, where he had been a sort of assistant editor, and had contributed articles on a wide range of authors, including Lewis Carroll, H.G. Wells, Coleridge, Byron and Sir Richard Burton. His new work, *Hieroglyphics*, is a treatise offering a literary theory, though that is too dry a description for its fervour: and it is also a work of fiction. Roger Dobson has pointed out the parallels between Machen's alter ego in *Hieroglyphics*, 'the Hermit', and Ambrose in 'The White People', and this fine shading between fiction and non-fiction is seen again in Machen's work, most dramatically in *The Bowmen*, and with tongue-in-cheek intention in his essay 'Dog and Duck'. It is used often enough to be a distinctive Machen device, years before the concept of 'metafiction' gave it literary credibility.

Hieroglyphics purports to record the discourses of a mysterious scholar, the Hermit, based on notes made by the narrator, one of the few visitors to his hidden haven:

> a big, mouldy house, standing apart from the street and sheltered by gaunt-grown trees and ancient shrubs; and just beside the dim and dusty window of the sitting-room a laburnum had cast a green stain on the decaying wall ... its black, straggling boughs brushed the pane, and on dark, windy nights while we sat together and talked of art and life we would be startled by the sudden violence with which these branches beat angrily upon the glass

This is a Gothic scene, Poe-derived, with the same frisson to it which will be found in the best haunted house stories, and it prepares the reader for the Romantic character of the Hermit, a reclusive dreamer in a desolate house, like Roderick Usher or Shiel's Prince

Zaleski. In his hollow, darkened room, candlelit, the walls hung with deep crimson which glows black and casts a heavy shadow, the Hermit seems indeed a strange figure, a sphinx, a nocturnal prophet who shuns the day, like Poe's Dupin, whom he evokes with approval.

In the intervals of silence, 'the inanimate matter about us found a voice, and the decaying beams murmured together, and ... the crypt-like odour of the cellar rose also into the room, mingling with a faint suggestion of incense, though I am sure my friend never burned it'. Machen is preparing us with this saturnine character and eerie scene as if in demonstration of the theory which is to be expounded: that the greatest literature is far beyond the ordinary and everyday, is rife with the strange and fantastic. The Hermit, be it noted, is not just a literary theorist but a mystic and visionary in the manner of Coleridge and De Quincey. One is reminded of Thomas Love Peacock's splendid spoof of Coleridge as 'Moley Mystic Esq', who lives on a dark island in a dark lake surrounded by dark trees, in a house named Cimmerian Lodge (*Melincourt*, Chapter thirty-one, 1817). There is even a hint that the supernatural lingers in the Hermit's rooms: 'I believe that once or twice we both saw visions, and some glimpses at least of certain eternal, ineffable shapes'.

In the first chapter of *Hieroglyphics*, the Hermit sets out the foundations of his faith, by asking how we distinguish between the many documents that use words. What defines true literature? he asks and answers, Ecstasy:

> If ecstasy be present, then I say there is fine literature; if it be absent, then, in spite of all the cleverness, all the talents, all the workmanship and observation and dexterity you may show me, then, I think, we have a product (possibly a very interesting one) which is not fine literature.

For ecstasy we may also read 'rapture, beauty, adoration, wonder, awe, mystery, sense of the unknown, desire for the unknown' and we find these in 'withdrawal from the common life and the common consciousness'. Poe, for example, may have written what seem mere detective tales, but his work suggests, 'the presence of that shadowy, unknown, or half-known Companion who walks beside each one of us all our days'.

In the second chapter, the Hermit expounds the purpose of

literature. It must give:

> that enthralling impression of the unknown, which is, at once,
> a whole philosophy of life, and the most exquisite of emotions
> ... you will find it in Celtic voyages, in the Eastern tale, where
> a door in a dull street suddenly opens into dreamland, in the
> medieval stories of the wandering knights, in Don Quixote,
> and at last in our Pickwick, where Ulysses has become a
> retired City man, whimsically journeying up and down the
> England of eighty years ago.

Journeying was important for Machen, from the long solitary rambles of his youth to the explorations of remotest London and his days as a 'strolling player'. In the suppressed chapter six of *The Secret Glory*, his character Ambrose Meyrick makes this explicit: 'We came very near to the ideal life which man was meant to lead. Who can measure the excellent effects of vagabondage, of the continual rolling which keeps the stone clean of moss and lichen?'.

It is to Rabelais, Cervantes and Dickens that the Hermit most often gives the laurels for true literature, but his dismissals are as entertaining as his enthusiasms. Jane Austen is 'a very keen and delicate, but very limited maiden lady'; George Eliot is 'poor, dreary, draggle-tailed', 'a superior insect'; Thackeray is 'a consummately clever photographer ... a showman with a gift of amusing, interesting "patter" ... an artificer of very high merit'. But by Chapter three, the argument is becoming too repetitive, too discursive, and we feel that by this time either the reader will not need more persuading or he will have become oppressed by the hammering home of the same point several times too many.

Despite this, *Hieroglyphics* won praise from those who were otherwise not greatly in favour of Machen's work, such as Algernon Blackwood, the writer of supernatural fantasy with whom he is often compared, and the art critic C. Lewis Hind, who recorded (*More Authors and I* 1922), 'I went frisking through it like a colt in a meadow, enjoying every page; then I went back to the beginning and read it all again carefully ...' and praised the book's 'sanity, insight and humour'. The theory of ecstasy as the touchstone of true literature won the approval of D.H. Lawrence in a passing reference to *Hieroglyphics* in an early letter (*The Letters of D.H. Lawrence*, Volume I, Cambridge University Press, 1979, 107). The occasional laboriousness aside, *Hieroglyphics* remains a handbook for those who acclaim the imaginative in literature, a polemic against the documentary and realist, and its air of the recondite, as if Machen is upholding a secret tradition, a lonely faith, an ancient order against barbarism and banality, adds to its appeal. This personal testament bears comparison with Arthur Symons's *The Symbolist Movement in Literature* (also 1899), the work which profoundly influenced Yeats, Eliot and Pound, in which Symons made a similar demand for literature: 'in this revolt against exteriority, against rhetoric, against a materialistic tradition; in this endeavour to disengage the ultimate essence, the soul ...' literature 'becomes itself a kind of religion, with all the duties and responsibilities of the sacred ritual'. Against the ponderousness and bombast of much Victorian literature popular and 'serious', Machen's work, like Symons's, charged the writer's craft with a new significance, and it was ironic that Grant Richards, the publisher who would not risk giving the public *The Hill of Dreams*, was much more willing to offer them the theory which underscored it: he published *Hieroglyphics* in 1902.

The metaphor of the hieroglyphic, used as a sigil signifying the high and hidden nature of everyday things, of even the most mundane lives, recurs in Machen's next work, the novella *A Fragment of Life*. It was another attempt at the Great Romance, the work which would finally convey what Machen wanted to say about the ineffable and unrecognised reality behind the surface of the material world: a return to the theme he felt he had inadequately expressed in *Clemendy*, *The Great God Pan*, and *The Hill of Dreams*. But this time Machen tried a different approach. Instead of the bachelor dandies and gourmets-of-the-curious of the Keynotes novels, or the lonely mystics of his more recent work, he deliberately chose the stock-in-trade characters of the conventional 'shopgirl romance' or sentimental novel of the day: a newly-married young respectable couple in a London suburb, with 'servant trouble', 'expectations' from relations, minor domestic dilemmas and entirely dutiful lives. In fact, Machen handles all this surprisingly well, with a fairly subtle undercurrent of irony which mocks only mildly, and does not have the bitterness found in *The Hill of Dreams* at the banality and hypocrisy of the townspeople. We are offered affectionate burlesque rather than biting satire.

And yet, there is more, of course, than this. Quietly at first, in fleeting asides, Machen gives us to understand that Edward Darnell the city clerk is sometimes moved by other considerations than his office work or household arrangements; he dreams at times of 'an ancient wood, and of a clear well rising into grey film and vapour beneath a misty, glimmering heat'; and sometimes, in glimpses of his wife Mary, he sees some unearthly, faunlike character in her; 'the grace of her form, and the brown hair, dropping over her ears and clustering in little curls about her neck, seemed to hint at a language which he had not yet learned'; 'he only dimly understood, but he could see the charm of her figure, the delight of the brown curls clustering about her neck, and he again felt that sense of the scholar confronted by the hieroglyphic'.

There is an especial poignancy about these passages describing the tenderness between Edward and Mary, and the pleasantness of their life together, for by this time his wife Amy was in the last stages of her illness, bedridden and beyond hope. Jerome K. Jerome gives a gentle account of these days in his memoirs:

> The memory lingers with me of the last time I saw his wife. It was a Sunday afternoon. They were living in Verulam Build-ings, Gray's Inn, in rooms on the ground floor. The windows looked out into the great garden, and the rooks were cawing in the elms. She was dying, and Machen, with the two cats under his arm, was moving softly about, waiting on her. We did not talk much. I stayed there until the sunset filled the room with a strange purple light.
> (JKJ 116 1926)

Perhaps we can only measure the depth of Machen's feelings for Amy if we take *A Fragment of Life* as an indication of what he would have wished their lives together to have been: certainly he never permitted himself to write directly about the matter.

At the end of the first chapter, having thrown out some hints that the Darnells have the potential for a richer interior life than their outward conformity implies, Machen states his theme explicitly. Although Darnell 'lived in the grey phantasmal world, akin to death, that has, somehow, with most of us, made good its claim to be life', yet this is only because he has 'forgotten the mysteries and the far-shining glories of the kingdom which was his by legitimate inheritance'. In a paradox he loved to return to, Machen insists it is what most 'sensible' people would call 'reality' that is actually the sham: the life of the numinous and wondrous is what we are really here to celebrate.

This is an article of faith for Machen. It is the key to all his finest writing, from *The Hill of Dreams* to *The Secret Glory*. He held to it with a tenacity worthy of the jaws of his ancient bulldog, Juggernaut. His belief in the eternal efficacy of ancient and solemn ritual, as a symbol of supernal truths, made him ever a High Churchman, but he believed more strongly still that there was spiritual significance in natural shrines, certain springs and groves and hills, and streams and stones; a pagan belief which was absorbed more freely by the early Celtic church, with its hermit or vagabond saints, than the more institutionalised Roman mission. In 'The White People' the girl's diary records the exploration of a landscape of evil, in which each feature has a sinister usage and meaning. In *A Fragment of Life* Machen attempts what may well be the harder task of depicting a landscape of spiritual beauty.

At the same time as he insists upon the superior reality of the transcendent, Machen is always at pains to point out that what we may think of as normal life is full of the bizarre and the enigmatic: and, in this novel, that is established by a gallery of rather Dickensian minor characters: the spiteful and grumbling old woman who thinks the Darnells' maid is not good enough for her son, but alternately welcomes and shuns her; the uncle whose liaison with an actress leads to the most picturesque subterfuges; and the aunt whose lunacy leads her to an obscure millenarian sect; the obsessive bargain-hunting of Darnells' neighbours. All these strange behaviours (none, in truth, all that much larger than life) contribute to Darnell's growing conviction that there is far more than the mere surface of things: 'there seemed to be gathering on all sides grotesque and fantastic shapes, omens of confusion and disorder, threats of madness; a strange company from another world'. By a cunning inversion, Machen asks us to agree that the emotions and motivations of people in the 'real' world are the really grotesque and fantastic things, not the high beauty and exultation which is known by the seeker of the sacred. The respectable people around him, like the labourers and prostitutes in their drunken cavortings in the London slum (in Chapter four of *The Hill of Dreams*), are unknowing participants in an infernal rite, frenzied and mindless and endless, symbolically. And, perhaps, actually, in the world that (according to Machen) lies behind this world.

In the final chapter of this short novel, the gradual awakening of the young couple to a more sublime apprehension of the world gathers pace and Machen's prose becomes stately and sonorous in the attempt to convey their new spiritual grace. Darnell's childhood memories of his family's origins in the far West (Gwent is not named but it is certainly intended) begin to revive strongly, and he relives visits to the venerable rambling house of his forebears, incidents in which their distant lineage among kings and saints still seems potent, and most of all wanderings in the land itself, the wild and secret domain. He begins to pore over the ancient manuscript heirlooms left to him by his father and to find the allegories in them a source of inspiration, as his clerkly life becomes more and more an irrelevance.

This was Machen's most lyrical and deeply-felt attempt so far to 'express the inexpressible' (as Sweetser puts it) and mostly it is only by image and symbol that he can speak to the reader of the vast difference between the material and everyday world and the realm of the spirit. The evocation of the land in the West, although it actually refers to Darnell's homeland and heritage, is meant to suggest too the mythical paradise that the ancients (and especially the Celts) placed in the West; Sarras, Atlantis, Avalon: 'only now and again in half-conscious moments or in sleep he had revisited that valley in the far-off west, where the breath of the wind was an incantation, and every leaf and stream and hill spoke of great and ineffable mysteries. But now the broken vision was in great part restored to him, and looking with love in his wife's eyes he saw the gleam of waterfalls in the still forest, saw the mists rising in the evening, and heard the music of the winding river'.

Machen uses too the resonant phrase, the memorable maxim or watchword, to win the reader's acquiescence. 'Man is made a mystery for mysteries and visions, for the realisation in his consciousness of ineffable bliss, for a great joy that transmutes the whole world' is one among a number of articles of faith he proclaims in the novel. But sustaining a conventional novel at such a sacramental level is hardly to be expected and so the novel ends rather abruptly with the admission that 'It would be impossible to carry on the history of Edward Darnell and of Mary his wife to a greater length, since from this point their legend is full of impossible events, and seems to put on the semblance of the stories of the Graal'. Later, in his autobiography *Far Off Things*, Machen records where the Darnell's new vision of life lead them:

> We went on our way by the river, and passed under Kemeys, a noble grey old house, with mullioned windows and Elizabethan chimneys. There is such a peace about this place, such a sweetness from the wood, such a refreshment from the water, so grave a repose upon it, that I translated to Kemeys one of my heroes, a clerk in Shepherd's Bush. This clerk had found out that all the bustle and activity of modern life are delusions and wild errors, and his reward was to be that he should end his days at Kemeys, sheltered from all turmoil and vanity, garnered from the evil world.

Kemeys, in the valley of the Usk just beyond Caerleon, still stands.

Some critics regard the novel's title as an admission that it is only a fragment of what Machen would have written if he could. But it has gradually become accepted as amongst Machen's most consummate achievements. Joshi (SJ 28-9 1990) exclaims, 'This is the Machen we love and admire: the writer who can invest the ordinary with a sense of numinous wonder'. It is certainly one of his most affirmatory works, a telling answer to those who see Machen as a rather too ingenious perpetrator purely of the dark side. M.R. James, for example, the master ghost story writer, expressed this aversion most pungently in a letter to a former student: 'Arthur Machen has a nasty after-taste; rather a foul mind I think, but clever as they make 'em' (Letter to Nicholas Llewelyn Davies, 12 January 1928). Dr James must certainly have been thinking of *The Great God Pan* and *The Three Impostors*, and might have been more charitable had he been more familiar with *A Fragment of Life*.

The story first appeared in *Horlicks' Magazine* in 1904, by courtesy of A.E. Waite, but received wider publication with its inclusion in *The House of Souls* (1906). It was issued under its own title in Secker's New Adelphi Library edition of Machen's books in 1928, but its low profile in the Machen canon continued until the present when its key position as Machen's 'first experiment in white rather than black magic' (DPM 16 1971) has gained it greater attention.

Machen wrote the first chapter of *Fragment* in the spring of 1899. But the rest of the book conveys something of an extraordinary episode of his life that followed the death of his wife Amy at the end of July in that year. He recorded in his autobiography only that 'a great sorrow which had long been threatened fell upon me: I was once more alone', and this reticence betrays the depth of his feelings. We can only surmise how far this bereavement, after a long and desolate period during which both must have been aware of an inevitable outcome, influenced his interpretation of the incidents he experienced in the following months, and which he recounts in chapters nine and ten of *Things Near and Far*, written over twenty years later.

Struggling for adequate terminology, Machen could only say that there was for him 'a singular rearrangement of the world'. He scented 'great gusts of incense' in the humdrum city streets of Holborn and Clerkenwell, felt himself literally 'walking on air', on a path that seemed to billow and bear him along, and in his Gray's Inn sitting-room he saw the pictures on the wall quiver as if they were about to 'dissolve and return into chaos'. This last experience came when, in a 'state of very dreadful misery and desolation and dereliction of soul', he tried 'a certain process' to gain mental relief. Following the vision of the pictures melting into the void, he felt swept by 'a peace of the spirit that was quite ineffable, a knowledge that all hurts and doles and wounds were healed', and in the days that came after he found everything, of the senses and of the spirit, 'an infinite and exquisite delight', so that he seemed in a very 'rapture of life'. Physical pains vanished at a touch, tiresome chores seemed no longer so.

This condition abided throughout the autumn and winter of 1899-1900, when it gradually faded into a strange medley of coincidences, meetings with strangers, odd echoes of his books. Machen is much less precise about this period, which he likens to changing from Syon, the paradisal city, to the fantastical Baghdad of *The Arabian Nights*, which he had read and relished in his young days.

In concluding his account of this time, in *Things Near and Far*, Machen begs to be spared the comments of the occultists who will tell him of a ready-made explanation out of Hinduism or the Kabbalah or the Tarot. But it is worth noting that the mystical state he describes is an almost classic account of the characteristics of similar experiences recorded in many ages and cultures, especially the quality of ineffability, the sense of things taking on a new significance, the transiency, the astonishment, or bewilderment at what has transpired, and the enhanced identification with all things encountered. (I summarise the characteristics in F.C. Happold's *Mysticism, A Study and an Anthology*, 1963.) To say that this is so does not purport to explain what Machen experienced, but only to place it in a wider dimension. Some have tried to work out what the 'certain process'

that Machen employed was — a form of self-hypnotism or meditation being the likeliest supposition — but ultimately this is scarcely
to the point. Others who have known a similar state, a similar
rapture, to that evoked with painstaking honesty by Machen, have
encountered it by other ways. The sceptic or agnostic will shrug, put
it down to psychological trauma, and pass on: those willing to accept
the possibility of a spiritual dimension to humanity will find
Machen's account a rich confirmation of the archetypes associated
with this dimension. Machen himself found it necessary, in evoking
the experience, to draw parallels with what is recounted in the
medieval legends of the Holy Grail, and in the lives of the Celtic
saints.

The influence of this experience on the mystical exaltation of the
Darnells in *A Fragment of Life*, in the Grail novels, *The Secret Glory*
and *The Great Return*, and in some later stories such as 'N', is clear
to see. Though Machen returned to the darkness, as he put it, the
recurrence of images from this time in his work testifies to its lasting
mark upon him.

It was during this period also that Machen joined the Order of the
Golden Dawn. In the final, exultant chapter of *A Fragment of Life* he
proclaims, 'The soul is made wise by the contemplation of mystic
ceremonies and elaborate and curious rites,' and it may have been a
desire to seek for more efficacious rites than those of the conventional church that led him, in this time of supreme inner turmoil, to
the occultism he in general regarded with scorn. The Order had been
founded in 1888 by Dr W. Wynn Westcott, purportedly by charter
from a German adept in Rosicrucian mysteries: this origin was
almost certainly bogus, or, to put it at its best, purely symbolic.
Nevertheless the techniques and ceremonies of the Order, mostly
composed by the gifted magical scholar McGregor Mathers, were an
inspired syncretism of elements from the Jewish Kabbala, Neo-Pla-
tonist philosophy, alchemical treatises and other sources: and they
were potent enough to attract and compel minds as questing and
diverse as W.B. Yeats, Algernon Blackwood, the actress Florence
Farr and Aleister Crowley, amongst many other writers and artists.

Machen was probably introduced to the Order by A.E. Waite,
whose authority as a researcher in the esoteric was growing and
whose *The Real History of the Rosicrucians* (1887) had caused something of a stir. His friendship with Waite, founded on vigorous
debating of each other's theories and a mutual respect mingled with

much badinage in a private mock-archaic language, was a mainstay for Machen in the months following the death of Amy, and it is possible that a sense of obligation to Waite was part of his motivation for joining the Golden Dawn. He chose the magical name of Frater Avallaunius, thus identifying himself with the dream figure in the Roman city recreated by Lucian in the fourth chapter of *The Hill of Dreams*. But he was never an important member of the Order, attaining only the second grade in its hierarchy, and he is dismissive of the episode in *Things Near and Far*, where he disguises it slightly as the Order of the Twilight Star. After commenting upon its fraudulent origins, Machen adds: 'But what an entertaining mystery; and, after all, it did nobody any harm'.

The Order of the Golden Dawn succumbed to schism and recrimination early in the new century, and Waite became a leading figure in a series of breakaway groups. Machen supported many of the new orders Waite founded, but probably in much the same spirit that he gave allegiance to various fraternal drinking societies. During one of the bitterest divisions between the rival occultists, in which Yeats had an acrimonious dispute with Crowley, Machen began to feel that *The Three Impostors* was coming to life: the pince-nez-wearing poet was the Young Man in Spectacles, pursued through London not by the sinister Dr Lipsius but by the equally malevolent Crowley. He alludes to this episode in chapter ten of *Things Near and Far*, along with other picturesque incidents, but he does not name the participants:

> I was once talking to a dark young man, of quiet and retiring aspect, who wore glasses — he and I had met at a place where we had to be blindfolded before we could see the light — and he told me a queer tale of the manner in which his life was in daily jeopardy. He described the doings of a fiend in human form, a man who was well known to be an expert in Black Magic, a man who hung up naked women in cupboards by hooks which pierced the flesh of their arms. This monster ... had, for some reason, ... taken a dislike to my dark young friend. In consequence, so I was assured, he had hired a gang in Lambeth, who were grievously to maim or preferably to slaughter the dark young man.

Yeats's deep interest in the occult has often been underplayed by commentators, even though it is a fundamental element of his work.

His *Autobiographies* (1955) attests to some experiences akin to Machen's. He too scented incense where none was likely to be, in his case on a train, and was filled with horror at the corruption of the faces he saw in the London streets, like Lucian Taylor in *The Hill of Dreams*. Though he lived for a time, as had Machen, upon bread and tea, he was more active in seeking out kindred spirits, and was a founder of the Rhymers Club, the coterie of poets who met at The Cheshire Cheese, an 'ancient eating-house' in Fleet Street. Machen's association with Yeats in the Golden Dawn seems to have spilled over into more general socialising during the early part of the century and in later years he tended to remember him with amused affection. Hilary Machen remembered his father reciting Yeats's 'The Folly of Being Comforted' (from *In the Seven Woods*, 1904) with reverence before a company of good friends, but adding 'And the extraordinary thing is that the great poet was one of the silliest men I have ever met'.

In 1902, having perceived that the period of serenity and strangeness which he characterised as like living in Syon and Baghdad had passed, Machen took the unusual step of becoming an actor. 'It is a very odd experience to go on the stage at the age of thirty-nine', he recalled in *Things Near and Far*, '... but it is a great entertainment'. Machen did not record what made him decide to try the stage as a career. Jepson (ME 55 1933) says he was 'seeking distraction from a great loss', meaning the death of Amy, although his wife had been an enthusiastic playgoer and habitué of theatrical gatherings. He was introduced to Frank Benson's touring Shakespearean Company by his fellow lodger Christopher Wilson, a close friend and the troupe's musical director: and Machen's great presence and naturally theatrical oratory were put to good use in minor, 'character' parts. He knew many of the players already through Wilson and relished the companionship and the bohemianism of the touring company. He always regarded these days as among the happiest of his life, though they were in fact quite brief, totalling about thirty-six months over a period of seven years from 1902-09, discounting several periods of 'resting'. The theatre was responsible for some lasting friendships and most especially for his introduction to his second wife.

Dorothie Purefoy Hudleston — the first name was not used — was the daughter of an Indian Army major, and a clergyman's daughter who died young, so that her youthful upbringing was with elderly aunts. She met Machen first through the musician Paul England, who gave her singing lessons and knew Machen well. 'The chief things I noticed', she recalled in her memoir, 'were Mr Machen's charming manners and his really beautiful spoken voice'. Purefoy was already distinctively bohemian in dress and attitudes, and she decided to go on stage with the Benson Company at about the same time as Machen. They were married at Marylebone Church in June 1903, Machen insisting upon describing himself in the official documentation, not as 'Author', but as 'Strolling Player'.

Machen gives his itinerary as an actor in letters to D.P.M. Michael in 1938 (SL 249 1988). He was with the Benson Company from January to June 1901 and then filled in with minor parts in music hall sketches, a farce and a melodrama for the remainder of the year. He worked in George Alexander's company at the St James Theatre and on tour throughout most of 1903, and returned to the Bensons during 1904. He took part in autumn tours in 1905 and 1907. In 'The Stroller', an essay for *Vanity Fair* in 1907, he recounts with some relish his experiences on the stage. His first appearance, as an extra in the crowd jeering Shylock (*The Merchant of Venice*) found him somewhat at a loss: 'Englishmen are not gesticulatory', he recorded, 'and when they do use gesture in common life, their gestures are usually horribly ungraceful; but when they try to use gestures on the stage, they are ridiculous, especially if they are new beginners'. (It is interesting incidentally, to note Machen deeming himself as an Englishman, one of the rare occasions when he overlooks his Welsh origins.) But despite this unpromising start, Machen enjoyed the Bensonians' Stratford-on-Avon season and had nothing but praise for the company, 'a sodality of old friends who had vagabonded over England together for ten years and upwards. They must have been something like a company of wandering craftsmen in the Middle Ages, with their sense of companionship and their sense of their craft'. When he left, because he needed better wages than the company could pay, his experiences were not always as cheerful, and he concludes his *Vanity Fair* article with a pungent summary of the sort of shabby practice he had witnessed, including bullying and swindling managers, dirty and dangerous backstages, and contemptuous employers; uncharacteristically, Machen's hatred of injustice goads him to urge his fellow-players to joint the Actors' Union, then in its early days. These strictures did not apply to his beloved Bensons, however, and he remained forever proud of his association with the company. Although he played only minor parts, he was equally fondly regarded by the company, many of whom remained friends once he had quitted the stage. Machen, with his love of the grand gesture and of medieval ceremony, was delighted when the company's founder and actor-manager Frank Benson was knighted on stage by George V at Drury Lane in 1916, using a property sword. Lady Benson, in her memoirs ten years later, imagined Machen as some great celestial spirit: 'I believe if I ever reach Heaven I shall meet him there, and he will be the same, and look the same; he will wear no halo like the angels, and if he has wings they will be concealed beneath a dusty old Inverness cape ... but he will be the friend of Saints' (*Mainly Players*, 1926).

Machen's farewell to the stage was as the Enchanter in Henry VI, Part II and gave occasion for some dramatic composition on his part which now, alas, seems to be lost. He told D.P.M. Michael in 1939: 'Shakespeare gives the magician's part simply as 'Conjuro te etc', I wrote up 'etc' to two or three pages of res. So far as I know, I am the only actor who ever wrote his own part in Shakespeare ... To conclude all fitly, I sent in my bill for this final performance at Stratford thus: 'To summoning Foul Fiend, Aschmoddai; jjs. To discharging same: jjs'. The business manager told me later that the Auditor of Accounts was a good deal puzzled' (SL 251 1988).

But the stage did not generally allow Machen to indulge in thaumaturgical writing and since the publication of *Hieroglyphics* in 1902 nothing more had appeared. However, Machen and Waite had composed a series of letters to each other couched in the obscure and allegorical language of alchemical texts, and Waite's publisher was sufficiently impressed by these to want to publish them. As the letters make references to secret orders, rites and journeys, they have been taken to possess great esoteric significance, and to relate in some way to the Golden Dawn. Only a handful of copies were published, as *The House of the Hidden Light* in 1904, with the majestic sub-title: 'Manifested and Set Forth in Certain Letters Communicated from a Lodge of the Adepts by The High Fratres Filius Aquarum and Elias Artista' — the 'fratres' were Machen and Waite respectively — and this book is thus second only to *Eleusinia* in its enticing scarcity for Machen collectors.

However, R.A. Gilbert has demonstrated beyond doubt (RAG 67-75 1987) that the letters, so far from bearing upon occult matters of signal import, were in fact in the nature of a private cipher for the two writers, used to celebrate their friendship in early 1902 with two much-desired maidens, known as 'the Shepherdess' and 'the Fair Wanton'. What we have is another splendid spoof, of the kind Machen always liked to indulge, half in earnest, half tongue-in-cheek: from *The Anatomy of Tobacco* to the pseudo-journalism of his later stories, he relished both outright hoaxes and works which blurred the borderland between fiction and fact. This delight extended too to a taste for elaborate mummery for he founded a drinking society, the Rabelaisian Order of Tosspots (we note the acronym) which used titles resurrected from *The Chronicle of Clemendy* (itself a mock translation) — Lord Maltworm, Lord Tosspot, etc — and resonant seeming rites devised by Machen. With Waite, he founded another, similar group, the Sodality of the Shadows (again the acronym is relevant), which also had elaborate rites, this time composed by Waite. The coffee clubs and tavern society of the Johnsonian age were assuredly part of the inspiration for these and other fraternities which Machen founded or frequented, but they were also a light-hearted living-out of Machen's constantly proclaimed dictum that all is ritual: and also of his insistence that the pleasures of the vine and the tankard, as also of the table, partake of the sacred too; he had no time for pallid asceticism, believing that the Puritan's self-denials were an abnegation adjacent to evil. ('I have always thought that he who neglects his belly will neglect his soul' he wrote to a friend in his seventies, echoing his revered Dr Johnson).

Perhaps the most notable of the drinking societies to which Machen belonged was the New Bohemians, which he joined in 1906 and frequented on and off until it faded away around 1914. It had been set up originally by the journalist T. Michael Pope and four friends, as a framework for tavern meetings in the outskirts of London — a walk followed by beer and talk. By the time Machen joined, the walking, as he observed wryly, was not much in evidence, and the company met mostly at the Prince's Head, Buckinghamshire Street, off The Strand, with occasional sojourns elsewhere in the heart of London. The group met each Thursday around a long table, and an old cigar box was passed around for members to place what money they could through a slot in the lid. The drinks were ordered, the coffer emptied, and the process repeated for subsequent refreshments. As Machen observed in his essay 'The Bitter Impatience' (1951), 'Not one of us had money in any solid sense, but some had (sometimes) a little more than others' and thus this amicable arrangement was a simple and effective form of commonwealth. The meeting would then proceed somewhat in a Pickwickian manner, with members proposing motions through the chairman, which would be vigorously and boisterously debated: 'We went at it hammer and tongs, till the tankards grew dry' Machen recalled. Amongst the members, Machen lists 'a journeyman tailor' who 'used to set our table in a roar with stories of the tailor's shop'; 'an Admiralty Official, a steady, stout good humoured fellow'; 'a city solicitor ... three or four journalists ... an officer of the Customs, a newspaper cartoonist, a novelist or two, a musician, an actor, a writer of "lyrics" for musical shows, and a few whose occupations remained a secret'. This motley crew included, indeed, the poet and essayist Richard Middleton (1882-1911), a particularly eager member, and his friend and Boswell, Henry Savage, himself a versatile author; Edgar Jepson, who published extracts from the society's minute-book in his memoirs; the novelist Edwin Pugh; and Cecil Chesterton, brother of G.K., a noted wit. Lord Alfred Douglas attended a few times but was not invited back: Arthur Ransome, in his journalist days before the success of his Lakeland children's adventure *Swallows and Amazons*, attended; Hilaire Belloc may have been an early member, as Savage recorded.

Middleton, struggling to sustain himself from sporadic payments for his verses and prose in various periodicals, took his own life with chloroform in a Brussels hotel in 1911, and was shortly after given acclaim as a tragic young Romantic poet, with a uniform set of his work published between 1912 and 1913. Machen wrote the introduction to *The Ghost Ship* (1912), an anthology of the best of Middleton's stories: the title story has a claim to being one of the finest humorous ghost stories in the language, with its spectral galleon that lands on a turnip patch in a quiet village and departs with added passengers, 'blazing with lights ... a noise of singing and fiddling on her decks'. Machen and Middleton had not entirely enjoyed each others' company, for Middleton did not like the discussion of abstruse liturgical points which Machen's presence at the New Bohemians was apt to inspire, whereas for his part Machen found Middleton inclined to be gloomy and take the debating too seriously.

Nevertheless, Machen wrote a full-hearted commendation of *The Ghost Ship*, describing the volume as 'an extraordinary book, and all the work in it is full of a quite curious and distinctive quality ... very fine work indeed' and concluding of the title story, 'I declare I would not exchange this short, crazy, enchanting fantasy for a whole wilderness of seemly novels ...'. Middleton's work is out of print today, but in its light and fanciful treatment of sometime sombre themes it invites comparisons to J.M. Barrie and other Edwardian writers for children, such as E. Nesbit.

It says something about both Middleton's and Machen's continuing neglect that H. Montgomery Hyde, a biographer of Wilde and chronicler of the nineties, credits Machen with the authorship of 'The Ghost Ship' in his biography of Lord Alfred Douglas (1984).

The significance of the New Bohemians in literary terms is perhaps not great, for few of its members are currently renowned to posterity, and Machen may have been premature in supposing it 'the last chapter in a very long, genial, and notable story; the story of the literary tavern life of London', for poets and artists were to gather again in the Fitzroy Tavern in the Thirties, and in various places subsequently. But the story of the society, as told by Savage and Jepson, is in itself of interest, regardless of the status of its members, and Machen was one of the main players in it. We admire the camaraderie and carousing, and wonder at the fates of those whose names are now sustained only by their belonging to such an insouciant fellowship.

Machen seems to have channelled most of his creative energy into the Waite collaboration, for he produced little else during the first few years of the new century. This hiatus will also have been partly due to his acting career, and to the sense of ending, and of beginning again, caused by the death of Amy, and the strange state of mind which followed this. The first work of any length he completed after emerging from this silence was also his most self-indulgent, and remains amongst his least-read. The book purports to be the 'Views and Principles' of an evangelical clergyman (again we note the preference for hoaxing) who praises everything Machen would damn, and vice-versa: and Machen's device is to let the pious Doctor condemn himself from his own mouth, by the sheer fatuousness of his arguments. It does not work well because Machen cannot identify himself sufficiently with his enemies, so we nowhere believe that any of them would propose the arguments he is satirizing. In *A Fragment of Life*, politics is included amongst those things of 'the grossest absurdity', 'matters in which men were never meant to be interested', since it makes them 'much like fair stones of an altar serving as a pigsty wall'. We are inclined to wish, after reading this polemic, that Machen had minded his own advice, for we find a man sufficiently conservative to prefer the South in the American Civil War, and to deplore democracy and universal education: while sufficiently radical to detest the bourgeoisie and the industrialist. Machen actually belongs in a long line of 'radical traditionalists' in English literature, from Cobbett and Peacock to Morris and Chesterton, men who united a love for the ancient and feudal and ceremonial with a distaste for the trappings of capitalism: but it is not advisable to go to this work, *Dr Stiggins*, for the best evidence of this.

Dr Stiggins was published under the obscure imprint of Francis Griffiths in 1906 and, as Sweetser says, 'was hardly noticed at the time and has received even less attention since' (WS 33 1964). It owed its origin to a preface Machen wrote for *The House of Souls*, an anthology of his supernatural stories which Grant Richards purchased en bloc and published in 1906. In the brief span of the preface, Machen's sardonic summary of Puritan achievements has a certain pungent power, but the mistake he and his publisher made was in thinking this could be sustained over an entire book. The preface is worth quoting though as an example of Machen in full flow in his role (as was once said of him) of a 'good hater':

> ... we know how Hampden died that England might be free, first under the martial law of the Great Protector, and afterwards under the Whig Oligarchy. We have read how Cromwell secured Representative Institutions from the attack of Tyrants, firstly by 'Pride's Purge', and then by the sterner, simpler method of abolishing the House of Commons ... We know how those foes of superstition hanged witches in Salem, how those friends of religious freedom flogged and hanged Quakers, how the enemies of the cruel Star Chamber caused the savage Indian to disappear from the land; while their allies at home baptized foals in cathedrals, hewed down the statues of the saints, shut up the theatres, and gave us the English Sunday.

Machen goes on to make a gloriously mocking case for his tales as suitable Sunday reading: in 'The White People', 'we see the necessity of the careful supervision of young females' and so on.

It was horror at the desecration and destruction of churches which later led to Machen's most notorious pronouncement on politics.

When asked to give his opinion for a *Left Review* pamphlet, *Authors Take Sides on the Spanish War* (1937), Machen declared he was and always had been for Franco, the protector of the Cross against those who would trample it down. He was in a very small minority (one notable ally was Wyndham Lewis) and one suspects that the editors specifically chose Machen to supply a view contrary to those of most of the British intelligentsia, to give the pamphlet a semblance of balance. But his apparent endorsement of the Falange should not be seen as representative of Machen's views as a whole: we should set against it his abiding detestation of respectability, prudery and commercial values, which make him far more of a maverick than some who would dismiss him as a blind conservative will allow. We have seen in *A Fragment of Life*, and shall see again in *The Secret Glory*, that his beliefs about 'the way of life that man was meant to lead' run completely counter to the conformism and work-ethic typical of the thinking of the Right.

The House of Souls collected three pieces which had previously only appeared in magazines, namely *A Fragment of Life*, 'The White People' and 'The Red Hand', and it reprinted the two Keynotes volumes, *The Great God Pan* and *The Three Impostors*, minus two stories and two linking episodes in the latter. The selection is a strong one (though 'The Shining Pyramid' could profitably have been preferred to 'The Red Hand') and Richards commissioned a frontispiece by Sidney H. Sime, the artist in black and white whose fantastical illustrations to Lord Dunsany's *The Gods of Pegana* (1904) had won much praise. Richards had correctly calculated that the reaction against the outré, which had followed the Oscar Wilde trials, had now subsided and some readers were ready to again to indulge a taste for the macabre.

If we review Machen's literary career at the end of 1906, with the publication of *The House of Souls*, we may well imagine his mixed feelings. True, with the anthology he was now the author of four commercially published full length books, discounting the translations and minor work. But on the other hand, he could only place his masterpiece *The Hill of Dreams* in the malted milk trade magazine edited by his old friend A.E. Waite: he had other work such as the *Ornaments* which had no outlet; he had no regular publisher; and he was far from well established in the world of literature.

Thomas Burke, later to win success with his stories of the Chinese in East London (*Limehouse Nights*, 1916, and others) and to express admiration for Machen's work, was just starting out in literature around this time. In *Son of London* (1947) he outlines the markets available to the aspiring writer just after the turn of the century. There were ten morning newspapers in London, and nine evening papers; around twenty monthlies, such as the *Strand*, *Pall Mall*, *Pearson's*, *Idler*; and about a dozen 'serious' journals, for example *The Athenaeum*, *The Nation*. At first sight, this seems to offer considerable opportunity for a literary journalist, probably far greater than today. But against this it is interesting to set Burke's list of the popular authors of the time, those who occupied the columns of all these publications and the lists of successful publishers:

> First in popular esteem were the neck-and-neck rivals, Hall Caine and 'Marie Corelli' ... Next to them came Rider Haggard, Anthony Hope, Conan Doyle, 'Seton Merriman', Stanley Weyman, Maurice Hewlett, Gilbert Parker, 'John Oxenham', E.F. Benson, Marion Crawford, Agnes and Egerton Castle, Israel Zangwill, S.R. Crockett, Jerome K. Jerome, Barry Pain, Pett Ridge, W.W. Jacobs, Mrs Humphrey Ward, Beatrice Harraden, Ellen Thorneycroft Fowler (etc) ... Above the lot of them towered Kipling. Henry James, George Moore and Yeats were the private property of the elect; ... and the advance-guard were talking of certain of the newer men who were not then widely known — Galsworthy, Chesterton, Bennett, de la Mare, Conrad, Belloc, W.H. Hudson, Maugham.
> (TB 182 1947)

Machen's distinctiveness from his contemporaries in literature may partly be judged by the few names in the above list, including those I have glossed as 'etc', whom he knew: only Jerome, a friend of Amy's, and Jacobs, probably as a friend of Jerome, though he was also very fond of Jacobs' humorous tales of old salts and village ancients. Chesterton and Belloc he may have met occasionally, Moore and Yeats he knew from the Order of the Golden Dawn. But that is all, and it is not the circle of a literary man-about-town.

Yet what a dusty catalogue of unregarded names it is. As Burke observed in 1947, 'only a few of them are read, or are readable today. Those who are still read are mainly the story-tellers. The most quickly forgotten were those who presented slices of contemporary life, not with too close fidelity, or "problems" which the years have solved' (TB 182 1947).

Against this background, it is perhaps easier to see why Machen took to the stage for his livelihood for a while. It may also help us understand why Machen's work still survives, getting on for one hundred years later. He did not concern himself with 'contemporary life' or the problems of the day. His works tell of eternal and elusive matters, questions of good and evil, reality and romance, beauty and strangeness. And they are written in the manner of Moore and Yeats, Chesterton and de la Mare, not of Caine and Corelli. The price for this was the consistent disregard of the public, and of publishers, no better demonstrated than by the fate of his next work, another attempt at the Great Romance.

Five: The Grail Seeker

In the final passage of *A Fragment of Life*, Machen described what happened next for the Darnells as having 'the semblance of the stories of the Graal'. And it was to the Graal — the Holy Grail — that his thoughts turned during a 'rest' from acting in 1906. He wrote to an old friend, Paul England, in February that year: 'I have been amusing myself lately by going to the BM [the British Museum] where I make researches into the origins of the Holy Grail legend to gratify a curiosity excited by Waite's ingenious but (I think) mistaken theory ... of the "Interior Church"; he would love to connect it with Cabalism, the Templars, the Albigenses' (SL 221 1988). Machen's researches continued for six months, taking in Celtic folk tales and saints' lives, the medieval romances from France, Germany and Italy, Malory's *Morte d'Arthur* and much more. He compiled a thick notebook of quotations, questions and wonderings, but without any conscious intention at the time of using the material in his writings.

Machen and Waite had worked together as early as 1903-4 on a verse drama, *The Hidden Sacrament of the Holy Graal*, which was published in Waite's *Strange Houses of Sleep* (1906) with a note that his collaborator wished to remain anonymous. The extent of Machen's contribution cannot be exactly known, though, as Gilbert has observed, no doubt he advised on the theatrical elements especially — in fact, he tried to interest the Benson Company in producing the play, unsuccessfully.

The legend of the Grail, and its many symbolic resonances, seized Machen's imagination, and Waite's parallel studies and theorising were a stimulus to him to form his own ideas as to its origin and meaning, mindful of the vastness of the theme: he called it 'one of the greatest problems and greatest complexes in literature'. He recorded his conclusions in several essays for *The Academy* and *T.P.'s*

Weekly, but his profoundest writings on the Grail are to be found in two novels, *The Secret Glory* and *The Great Return*.

The first of these was written mostly in 1907, though it used fragments from as early as the 1890s. Episodes from the novel (Machen preferred to call it a 'Romance') were published in *The Academy* in 1907-8, and the first two chapters appeared in *The Gypsy*, a journal founded by Machen's fellow New Bohemian Henry Savage in 1915-16, as part of an intended full serialisation: but *The Gypsy* did not last that long. The work did not find book form until 1922 when Martin Secker published it in response to the growing interest in Machen's work: but even then it lacked two chapters which Machen decided to suppress. *The Secret Glory* was reprinted twice as part of sets of Machen's work, but has not otherwise been revived, and no paperback has ever been produced.

If we consult even those critics who are sympathetic to Machen, we may not find this neglect surprising. Reynolds and Charlton note that 'much of the book is palpable patch-work', that 'Machen must have taken great pains in his effort to make the mystical and religious parts ring sound. It is unlikely, however, that many readers will think he succeeded' and that it is 'sadly not the book it could have been' (RC 103-5 1963). Wesley Sweetser calls the book 'half satire, half mysticism ... imperfectly blended' and finds the satire 'charged with rancour and bias' (WS 33 1964) while Michael similarly characterises it as 'an unsuccessful attempt to fuse two main themes that lack congruity' (DPM 35 1971). Finally, Joshi has the same objection: 'the work does not hang together. [It] is too unfocused, too desultory' (SJ 31 1990).

The plot and the narration of *The Secret Glory* may indeed seem unpromising. In essence, we witness the youthful turmoils of a schoolboy mystic, a jejune bohemian, reacting savagely against the philistine and materialist regime of his public school, holding true instead to a vision of art and mysticism which has its origins in his upbringing in wild Gwent. The boy, Ambrose Meyrick, an avatar of Machen, reads Rabelais, reveres the memory of his dead father and has only contempt for his guardian-uncle-and-headmaster in one, the sanctimonious and scheming Horbury.

The narration is certainly fragmentary, sometimes directly describing events, more often quoting from various indistinct memoirs, and from Meyrick's notebooks and other works. In his letters Machen repeatedly refers to the book as an 'experiment', but if he meant by this the device of telling the story from a collection of different perspectives, then it must be conceded this does not work well, and may only leave the reader muddled.

Yet for all these defects, *The Secret Glory* remains a book that changes lives. Perhaps the most notable example of this is to be found in John Betjeman's verse memoir *Summoned By Bells* (1960). Cycling the lanes of Cornwall after ugly quarrels with his father ('Yes, I'm in trade and proud of it, I am! ... I'll keep you at it as I've kept myself') he came to the small, secluded church of St Ervan, where he shared evensong and tea with the Rector, who lent him Machen's book: 'I would not care to read that book again./It so exactly mingled with the mood/Of those impressionable years ...'. Inspired by the book, the fifteen-year-old Betjeman made pilgrimages to holy wells and ancient chapels and felt that 'Somewhere among the cairns or in the caves/The Celtic saints would come to me...'. Later, responding to the appeal fund for Machen in his old age, Betjeman averred, 'I really do owe Arthur Machen more than money can show. His *The Secret Glory* sent me Anglican when a Public School Evangelical aged 15 ...' (MS 3 1988).

Winchester public schoolboy Colin Summerford, also at fifteen, had a similar response to the book, and in his seventies he still thought it 'the finest and richest of Machen's works'. 'The core of this unique book', he wrote, 'lies in its mystical and visionary scenes witnessed by Ambrose Meyrick ... These passages are written with the utmost conviction ... I do not know of any book, save Holy Writ, which has the same spiritual intensity' (essay in *Aklo*, a journal of the fantastic, winter 1990-91). The author Frank Baker found even just the title, with its suggestion of a summoning to a shared ideal, was of profound significance for him.

For these, and for others, the two elements of the novel, the attack on the public school ethos, and the ardent defence of an ancient and now hidden faith, are not so incongruous as the critics claim. By offering both rebellion against an established order and a chivalric allegiance to a lost cause, an honourable tradition, *The Secret Glory* appeals to two very potent emotions and motivations. Furthermore, to use a religious analogy, (as Machen often does) Lupton, Meyrick's detested public school, is the Babylonish captivity he must endure before he reaches Jerusalem: its part in the book as the symbol of the trials and endurances the Grail seeker must undergo is as essential as the supernal visions Meyrick is granted.

Machen's reason for choosing the public school as the representative of all that is anathema to his ideals is often cited as the churlish treatment inflicted by the pupils of Harrow upon the troupe of actors, of whom Machen was one, who had come to perform a play for the school, for they were jeered at and jostled and generally subjected to scorn. This incident no doubt aided Machen's vituperations, but he gives the particular cause in a letter to Vincent Starrett in 1919: 'The venom is extracted from a chance reading of the life of one Bowen, a famous Harrow master. The point of view annoyed me; and the annoyance got into my book. Bowen, by the way, was famous as a writer of Harrow School songs: nauseous muck, most of them'. Whatever his immediate motive, there is no doubt that the public school is an excellent catch-all for many of the things Machen despised: the puritanical 'Muscular Christianity' which shunned ritual and mystery; the emphasis on worldly success; the insistence on conformism and a bogus 'team spirit' that suppresses individuality; and the crassness that raises prowess at futile sports far above aesthetical discernment. Machen's satire of all this is written with great relish and 'a really wicked skill', as Reynolds and Charlton concede: and it must be borne in mind that at this time the prestige of the public schools was largely inviolate, chronicled in fiction only by the likes of H.A. Vachell's *The Hill* (1905), which a modern commentator has called an 'unashamedly sentimental, snobbish and patriotic' paean to Harrow (Peter Parker, *The Old Lie: The Great War and the Public School Ethos*, 1987): Alec Waugh's *The Loom of Youth*, the first serious attack, did not come until 1917. Far from being an unwelcome distraction from the mystical passages of the book, the public school satire is an integral element, a necessary counterpoint and, in all its sardonic splendour, a highly entertaining blast against a wholly deserving foe.

Nevertheless: it is Ambrose Meyrick's experiences of spiritual ecstasy and his devotion to a hidden ideal that inspire readers of the book so profoundly. And to these we must now turn.

The second chapter of the book is in a completely different key to the first. Having thoroughly established the vulgarity and dishonesty of Ambrose's public school, Machen brings us to a contrasting vision of the utmost grace and sanctity. In a mystical reverie, the schoolboy beaten for staying out after hours to visit a Norman abbey seems to drink from the dark and glittering waters of a holy well and finds himself in a torchlit procession to a great church on a hill, then, with a sudden transformation, pilgrimaging alone through a vast forest to a remote chapel, where he witnesses an old man and two acolytes serving a Mass for a most high, hidden and holy object. As the vision ends, he hears a voice proclaim his fate for this glimpse of the exalted and sacred secret.

This mere outline can convey nothing of the majestic splendour of Machen's prose in these passages, which has a claim to be amongst the most beautiful writing he achieved. The American commentator Maude Hazelton claimed, 'For sheer beauty in English prose I know of nothing to compare with Machen's description of the vision of the Grail vouchsafed to Ambrose Meyrick ... except, perhaps, De Quincey's "Dream-Fugue"' (*The Cup and Arthur Machen*, Kansas City, 1923). It should be noted that Machen nowhere until the very end of the book states outright that Meyrick's quest is that of the Grail, though he uses motifs and images from both the medieval legends and earlier tales which tell of a numinous vessel of supreme sanctity.

In later chapters, Ambrose recalls his boyhood visits, with his father, to the broken and overgrown shrines of the Celtic saints, Ilar, Cybi, Teilo, and in particular a journey to a white-walled farmhouse where lives the last hereditary keeper of a precious relic of St Teilo, a cup which legend holds he brought back from paradise. Few now come to see the cup, but Ambrose and his father kneel with the old man who preserves it, and recite an ancient Welsh chant. We see that this humble ritual is the source of Ambrose's vision, the enactment in this world of the supernal apotheosis he experienced in vision. Machen's evocation of the Celtic legends told to Ambrose by his father is poetic and authentic, echoing the richness and strangeness of the early bardic tales and utterances: not before, in fact, had Machen revealed the depth of his intimacy with and pride in his Welshness.

As with *A Fragment of Life*, Machen has difficulty in carrying on the account of his character once his consciousness of the rapture which is the great reality has been fully and stirringly established. The ending of *The Secret Glory* is equally abrupt. Meyrick, having been entrusted with the return of St Teilo's treasure to a sanctuary in Asia, is captured by Muslim brigands on his way back and murdered in a mock crucifixion: all this told in a few paragraphs. This rather too convenient, unconvincing and crude finale does the book a grave disservice, and has probably played a major part in diminishing its stature both among Machen's works and generally.

But before reaching this unfortunate epilogue, Machen introduces a third theme, along with the public school satire and the Grail mysticism, which is less often noted. This is a celebration of bohemianism, represented in *The Secret Glory* by an episode which may otherwise seem curiously out of place, when Ambrose escapes with the young school maid, Nellie, for a secret holiday in London, mingling with poets and artists, and visiting Soho haunts which Machen describes with a gusto that suggests they come from memory not invention: the Café called Chateau de Chinon, and a splendid old tavern, the Three Kings. In this segment of the novel, too, we find a long extract from Ambrose's notes towards his book, *In Defence of Taverns*, which Machen uses as a vehicle for his musings upon the significance of the symbol of the Vine, and the Cup, and of how the 'sad neglect of the Dionysian Mysteries' is driving all inspiration from the world.

Yet, enjoyable those this part of the book is, it does not represent the soul of *The Secret Glory*, that essence which has drawn so fervent a response from some readers. This may be found in another of Ambrose's meditations, and it speaks for Machen as well as his character:

> ... the Celtic Church was the Company of the Great Errantry, of the Great Mystery, and, though all the history of it seems but a dim and shadowy splendour, its burning rose-red lamp yet glows for a few, and from my earliest childhood I was indoctrinated in the great Rite of Cor-arbennic. When I was still very young I had been humoured with the sight of a wonderful Relic of the Saints — never shall I forget that experience of the holy magic of sanctity. Every little wood, every rock and fountain, and every running stream of Gwent were hallowed for me by some mystical and entrancing legend, and the thought of this High Spiritual City and its Blessed Congregation could, in a moment, exorcise and drive forth from me all the ugly and foolish and gibbering spectres that made up the life of that ugly and foolish place where I was imprisoned.

The Celtic Church was for Machen the great lost cause, the secret faith that gave shape to his yearning for the land of Gwent. Never at ease with the Anglican church, but with reservations also about Latin catholicism, he found in the legends surrounding the saints of the early British church the validation of his own deeply felt conviction that Christianity is 'the greatest of all Mystery Religions'. He was proud of its origin independent from the Roman mission sent by Pope Gregory in the seventh-century to convert the Anglo-Saxons, and its distinctive character, caused by the fusing of hagiology and mythology.

When the Celtic spirit was much in the air, in the 1890s, Machen does not seem to have allied himself to the movement. Yeats and, adoptively, Lionel Johnson for Ireland, 'Fiona Macleod'/William Sharp for the Gael, Ernest Dowson's Breton idylls, even Arthur Symons's Cornish roots, were all taken as evidence of a Celtic renaissance, along with the work of a host of minor writers: but Machen did not at this time put in his claim for the Welsh. His Nineties tales — *The Great God Pan, The Three Impostors* — were cosmopolitan in tone, and even Gwent settings were apt to be referred to only vaguely as 'the West'.

But by the new century, Machen seems to have been ready to make known his own allegiance to, and understanding of, the Celtic spirit, exemplified by the early Celtic Church. And he was enabled to put forward his views in essays for *The Academy*, a journal edited by Lord Alfred Douglas, the notorious friend of Wilde, a poet and litigant who was an admirer of Machen's work and appointed him to write on religious themes for his periodical. Douglas was later to recall that Machen's contributions were instrumental in his decision to convert to Rome. In three essays on 'The Sangraal', and a fourth responding to the arguments of Alfred Nutt, another Grail researcher, Machen proposes the theory that underlies *The Secret Glory*, that the Grail was a relic of a Celtic saint, and the Grail legends may be the remembrance of the lost liturgy of the Celtic church.

Machen deals in characteristically brusque fashion with a number of other theories as to the significance of the Grail, current in his time. The anthropological school, which sees only fertility rites or sun mythology, gets short shrift as too reductionist. Sebastian Evans's ingenious allegorical explanation, which finds exact parallels between the Grail legends and events in thirteenth century England, is acknowledged as skilfully worked out, but dismissed on the good grounds that some Grail romances predate this period, and because there is nothing to account for the loss of the Grail. The involvement of the Knights Templar, always a favourite panacea of occultists, is also found wanting for cogent reasons. And then Machen advances his own cautiously-worded theory: 'the Legend of the Graal, as it may be collected from the various Romances, is the glorified version of early Celtic Sacramental Legends, which legends had been married to certain elements of pre-Christian myth and folk-lore'.

In identifying the pagan elements in the Grail legends, Machen notes that the Quest element probably derives from the voyages of Celtic heroes, such as Arthur, to the otherworld, in search of some great magical treasure, but he stresses too that this is not foreign to the Celtic Christian tradition:

> Celtic 'monk-errantry' is a strange matter; one does not know how far these voyages were the expression of missionary zeal, how far they were due to the desire for a greater solitude than might be had in the cell, for the 'desert in ocean' that St Columba's monk tried to discover, or how far they were really voyages to the semi-pagan, semi-Christian paradise, deep Avalon of the apple-blossoms far beyond the waves, the Glassy Isle where, some say, Merlin is hidden, having with him the Thirteen Rarities of Britain. In these voyages, undoubtedly, we have the origins of all that is most poetic and most romantic in the romances of chivalry; and the journeys of the Celtic monks may well have had some share in the Quests of the Knights of the Graal.

Machen develops his theory further by pointing out the devotion given to the sacral objects associated with Celtic saints, such as their bell, book or crozier, and that the nature of the Grail in the various legends is not always, or even mostly, a cup: in some there is a suggestion it is a stone. Could it not be an altar stone? After drawing parallels between the legends of St Joseph of Arimathea, who is claimed to have brought the Grail to Glastonbury, and St David, whose altar, Sapphirus, was one of the treasures of Glastonbury Abbey, Machen speculates upon what Mass the Celtic church used, and notes that it probably derived from Gallic, and ultimately Byzantine rites, and differed from the Roman liturgy therefore in a number of ways, but most significantly in an invocation to the Holy Spirit during Eucharist. The Grail legends invariably include a vision in which there is a descent of the Holy Spirit at the attainment of the Grail. Bringing all these elements together, Machen makes out a scholarly and inspired case for the legends of the Grail as remembrance of the celebration of the Celtic Mass, suppressed when the

Roman church achieved dominance throughout Britain following the Synod of Whitby (664 AD), and now lost.

In its recognition of the predominant importance of the Celtic elements in the Grail legends (as distinct from English, Norman and Provencal elaborations on the theme), and its careful consideration of the parallels with the lives of the Celtic saints, usually regarded as 'historically worthless' but nevertheless, as Machen knew, full of rich significance for the understanding of Celtic culture, Machen's theory was ahead of its time. Even if we do not accept every component of his argument, there can be no doubt that it is worthy of respect, research and refinement: it does not stand with the British Israelite, Gnostic Sect or Templar Conspiracy schools of thought. The Celtic Mythos, as he elsewhere called it, was to remain a highly-charged personal metaphor for Machen. He encapsulated it once more in reviewing Waite's *The Hidden Church of the Holy Grail* for *T.P.'s Weekly*, another journal for which he became a regular contributor in 1909. After faithfully reporting Waite's view that the Celtic elements in the Grail legends are mere accidents, distilled by the minstrels and monks who wrote the medieval romances from the 'faint and distant rumour' of the Celtic tales, but without any deep understanding of them, Machen gives the most succinct summary of his detailed ideas on the theme:

> Personally, I am of the opinion that the story is of Celtic origin, and that the Knights of the Graal are Welsh saints in armour. A relic of peculiar sanctity — a portable altar, perhaps — used by St David, and famed for its miraculous properties, became confused at a very early period with the Magic Cauldron of pagan tradition; the ruin of the Celtic church and the Celtic State found its symbolism in the desolate 'enchantment' of Britain; the loss or concealment of the relic became the vanishing of the Grail ...

One of Machen's last contributions to *The Academy* was 'a bit of wreckage from the later part of *The Secret Glory*', as he later described it. 'In Convertendo' concerns Ambrose's return to the Wern, his father's old home in Gwent, now tenanted by a scholarly and eccentric cousin and his daughter, Sylvia. This passage is another finely wrought evocation of Gwent, both in its actual landscape and its symbolic significance as the domain of the Grail. There were in fact two entire chapters of such 'wreckage', which were not included in

The Secret Glory as published. In 1918, Machen wrote to his American champion Vincent Starrett: 'If you will give me your faithful word not to print, or allow anyone else to print, or allow anyone the mere opportunity of printing, I will send you the originally designed conclusion of *The Secret Glory*; a failure, but a singular experiment' (SM 37 1977). Two years later, after a delay caused by Machen's nervousness at sending the package during and just after wartime, the cancelled chapters were sent to Starrett, Machen adding only, 'I have forgotten what most of it means'. The manuscript passed through various other hands before ending at Yale University Library. S.T. Joshi arranged for copies to be made for circulation among Machen scholars in the 1980s, and in 1992, by permission of the author's estate, the suppressed writing was published. The effect of the chapters is to fill in some of the gaps between Ambrose's departure from Lupton and his death, which is unchanged by the missing work. We learn more about his time at the Wern, and as a strolling player, but more especially, in a highly ethereal and elusive section, we see Ambrose and Sylvia joined in a spiritual marriage involving a vigil before the sacred relic kept at the old farmhouse. Again, some of Machen's prose reaches his highest attainment in the lyrical evocation of Gwent country and of mystical experience: what Machen had discarded many lesser writers would have regarded as the furthest reach of their art. The Celtic motif remains strong and clear in this section too, with more tellings of legends and tales, and imitation of the sonorous pronouncements of the bards. And yet one can see why Machen rejected the chapters, for while they enhance, they do not advance the book's theme, and he may have judged that he was already expecting the average publisher and public to tolerate a good deal more mysticism than they were commonly inclined to accept in a 'novel'. Even without the extra sections, *The Secret Glory* took fifteen years to get into print, and then only on the crest of a great wave of Machen enthusiasm.

While this most deeply-felt personal testament was still in manuscript, therefore, Machen saw his opportunity to express the essence of the Grail theme when, as a journalist on the *Evening News* during the Great War, his visionary fantasies gained an eager readership (see Chapter six). Although *The Great Return*, his second Grail novel, did not sell well in book form, it had already been published in the columns of the newspaper, towards the end of 1915. The symbolism and the assumptions underlying *The Great Return* are the same as those of *The Secret Glory*, but they are more gently and allusively conveyed, and the later story has a satisfying unity which makes the reader more at home with the theme. The journalist narrator visits 'Llantrisant, the little town by the sea in Arfonshire' because of certain odd reports he has heard. We share in his gradual unfolding of a supreme spiritual renewal which has descended on this quiet domain. Great radiances are seen at sea, sacral incense pervades the air even in the dissenting chapels, the hopelessly sick are returned to vigour, sworn enemies end their feuds. Mysterious strangers, called by the local people 'the Fishermen' are seen, and their presence strikes great awe in the witnesses. For a period of nine days 'it was as if one walked the miraculous streets of Syon', Machen reports: and we note the use of the term he used to describe his own time of wonder at the turn of the century. The conviction, the exultant cadences, Machen achieves in this short novel are successful where they might have been merely cloying or pious, and it is likely he was writing in part from the strength of his own experiences. But, as he later told friend and fellow-author Oliver Stonor, there were other influences: his love of the Pembrokeshire countryside around Tenby, which, as the destination of numerous holidays, was beginning to take on some of the potency of Gwent; the recollection of a Welsh religious revival a few years earlier, which had been accompanied by sightings of spontaneous lights; and Mrs Oliphant's novel, *A Beleaguered City*, in which the dead stage a ghostly insurrection against the immorality of the living (A & M 31-2 1986).

The Great Return was Machen's last proclamation of the Grail, and one of the reasons it works so well is that one senses it is a dream of wish-fulfilment for Machen, long the exile from his land, long the seeker for a spirituality that satisfied his own burning certainties about the presence of wonder all around us. All of the strange occurrences in the novel are but harbingers of the Great Return of the title, the Return of the Grail. But perhaps the greatest miracle is the response of the people, who do not shun the wonders or try to deny them, but recognise them for what they are. Would the people really react in this way? The question is not answered directly, but it is clear that Machen did believe the Celtic spirit was still alive and undiminished, despite, as his narrator enumerates, 'the wave of the heathen Saxon ... then the wave of Latin medievalism, then the waters of Anglicanism; last of all the flood of their Calvinistic Methodism, half Puritan, half pagan ...'; despite these, in Machen's fervent hope, the Grail would indeed still be acclaimed.

Though he did not succeed in making the major work, the Great Romance, out of the Grail legends, Machen's contribution to the literature and the scholarship of this most enduring of symbols is deserving of greater recognition. Twenty-five years after his researches in the British Museum, the remembrance of the Quest was still vivid for Machen. Thanking A.E. Waite for a copy of his new study, *The Holy Grail*, he recalled the 'many adventures of body and spirit undertaken together in the gardens and the halls of Camelot in the days that were' (SL 53 1988).

1. The High Street, Caerleon, at the turn of the century.

2. Kemeys House, one of the local houses which haunts Machen's writing.

3. Llanddewi Church, at which Machen's father was rector.

4. Bertholly House, prototype of many of Machen's atmospheric houses.

5. Twyn Barlwm Mountain: 'The Hill of Dreams'.

6. S.H. Sime's frontispiece to *The Hill of Dreams* (1907).

8. At his favourite home, in St John's Wood.

7. Machen and his second wife, Purefoy.

9. At dinner with Lady Constance Benson and Sir Max Beerbohm.

10. Autographed portrait in character as Dr Johnson, a favourite rôle.

11. Machen during his time in Fleet Street.

Six: The Herald of St George

Acting was an irregular and unreliable career, while the rewards for literature had always been minimal, and Machen, after the lukewarm response to what he knew to be his masterpiece, *The Hill of Dreams*, had experienced another fallow period for his books when, in 1910, he accepted employment with the *Evening News*. He was at first used for all-round reporting duties of a trivial kind which he found intolerable — interviewing the famous he found embarrassing — but was gradually allowed to become an acknowledged feature writer on favourite subjects such as traditions and ceremonies, the byways of London, and religious matters, as well as doing book reviews. Nevertheless, he loathed the feeling of obligation that being a waged employee implied, and bitterly resented the, at times, dismissive treatment given to his work, especially in the later years.

Purefoy Machen recalled: 'Though at first they nearly worked him to death, he liked the Editor, a Mr Evans, and made some good friends ... Arthur remained with the *Evening News* for eleven years, but the later ones were not pleasant ... The paper did have one merit, however, it paid good salaries, so it was lucky that my son chose to arrive while Arthur was so employed' (PM 66-7 1991).

In retirement, Machen recalled for Oliver Stonor his working environment. 'I can remember smiling such a grim inward smile, on many a morning as I sat in the Reporter's Room ... writing 'a nice column of descriptive', three telephones telephoning, four reporters differing, five sub-editors sub-editing, one News Editor cursing: and Kennedy Jones's face at the door' (A & M 30 1985). The last named, a former editor of the paper, was a despised general henchman of the boorish and philistine proprietor, Lord Northcliffe. Machen's contribution to *The Book of Fleet Street* (1930) emphasises the constant demand of the deadline, requiring him to write finished descriptions of events even as he witnessed them, and he recalls in particular covering several capital trials at the Old Bailey, the Battle of Sidney Street, the funeral of a Crimean War veteran and the coronation of King George V. But he was not always at such momentous scenes, and he also lists the bizarre variety of chores he might be assigned, including reporting on a billiards match, new bell buoys, a lost donkey, Dutch eel boats, a poltergeist, chatting with the actor Beer-bohm Tree aboard a liner off the Pembroke coast, and interviewing an old chair-repairer. 'The day after', he adds, 'I am shot down in a bucket a great number of feet into the subterranean workings of the Tube'. The paper also sent him on expeditions to the provinces, including the mining districts of Yorkshire, Durham and South Wales (1912); to Somerset (1913); Ulster (1913); East Anglia (1915) and various cities for a series 'Saturday Nights in Wartime'; Sheffield, Birmingham, Leeds, Leicester. Machen did his best to overcome his antipathy to industrial sprawl. There is no doubt that his journalistic career did much to enrich Machen's experience, but his pleasure was almost always marred by the harrying necessity to get his copy in by deadline before being told of his next assignment.

This high profile position with the *Evening News* inevitably in-creased awareness of Machen as a writer and as a 'character'. He was in effect a 'star' journalist on a major newspaper with a wide and cosmopolitan readership and he was bound to come to the notice of many more people than his literature had ever commended. He became a familiar Fleet Street figure, as journalist St John Adock recalled:

> You might run across him any day of the week at Ludgate Circus, in Fleet Street and the purlieus of Whitefriars, and his very unlikeness to the multitude round about him gave you a feeling that he belonged there ... his sturdy form and gait are vaguely reminiscent of Dr Johnson, but, instead of a wig, from under his small felt hat his thick iron-grey hair streams down stiff as wire. To set eyes on him thus, especially if the weather was not too mild for him to be enveloped in his great cape-overcoat, warmed you with a feeling that life had not yet been reduced quite to a dead level, that the free Bohemian spirit which quickened the world of literature in its golden age was not yet extinct, nor the glorious individuality of Fleet Street wholly departed from it.
> (ASA 213 1928)

This Johnsonian comparison may be seen also in an article by Oliver

Warner, recalling the Fleet Street days, in *The Bookman* of March 1932. Machen's acting career, he notes, 'has left a curious legacy — a deep and resonant voice ... and a Johnsonian aspect. Voice and aspect are the resolution, the synthesis of a rare personality. Johnson would have approved his conversation. It is full of erudition, borne without a trace of pomposity, and embracing a wide and various range of subjects; it is kindly; it is humorous and it is opinionated'.

So well established was the Johnsonian identification that Machen was commissioned to play the part, with impromptu repartee, for a private dinner party, and thoroughly enjoyed himself, and in 1922 he took the part in a film of Old and New London which however was never released, and now seems lost.

Despite the affection which he seems to have inspired, Machen always recalled his days as a journalist with a cold fury, but they were not completely unproductive from a literary standpoint. As we shall see, a later editor, Alfred Turner, encouraged him to write his memoir, which was serialised in the newspaper as 'Confessions of a Literary Man' and published in book form as *Far Off Things*: many regard it as amongst his finest work. The paper also serialised two novellas and some religious meditations, all three finding subsequent book publication. But most of all, it was in the *Evening News* that Machen's most successful and famous piece of fiction of his entire career appeared.

It was a brief tale, telling of a single supernatural incident, but for years afterwards it was indelibly associated with his name: even today, it is the likeliest point of contact with his work for the general public.

'The Bowmen', published in the *Evening News* of September 29 1914, was Machen's response to the news from the front of the retreat of the British Army from Mons, a courageous and costly rearguard action against considerable odds. In the thick of the fighting, a young soldier inconsequentially remembers the motto on a plate in a vegetarian restaurant (Machen does not miss the opportunity for a light dig at lentil cutlets): *Adsit Anglis Sanctus Georgius* ('May St George be a present help to the English'). He finds himself uttering this aloud as the enemy advances.

The roar of battle dies away, but the saint's name is taken up a thousand-fold by a throng that appears to the fore: 'a long line of shapes, with a shining about them. They were like men who drew the bow, and with another shout, their cloud of arrows flew singing and tingling through the air towards the German hosts'. The assailants fall by the thousands: their generals decide the English must have used some new poison gas, 'as no wounds were discernible on the bodies of the dead'.

Machen thought his story 'an indifferent piece of work' and later identified its inspiration as Kipling's 'The Lost Legion' (from *Many Inventions*, 1893) in which a British force in Afghanistan has assistance from the ghosts of dead soldiers. This 'got mixed with the medievalism that is always there' (in his head) and so his own story was made. He is over-modest as usual, for, although the story's status as propaganda and morale-booster must limit its literary qualities, it is nevertheless quietly effective, sparingly written and with a certain chivalric appeal, like an episode from Malory or Henry V.

Light, a Spiritualist magazine, reported Machen's story in its issue of 10 October 1914, calling it 'a remarkable piece of imaginative word-painting' and thus making plain that the story was fictional. The other leading journal in the field, the *Occult Review*, wrote to Machen and was assured by him that the story had no foundation in fact. Parish magazines asked if they could reprint the story, and Machen agreed. It was clear the story excited interest and Machen may have been bemused, and rather gratified, at its success. But he was hardly prepared for what followed.

By a process which can now only be conjectured, but which is evident again and again in the diffusion of folklore, the story and variations upon it began to be repeated as fact, and by the spring of 1915 the assertion that there was indeed supernatural intervention at Mons gained widespread credence. In sermons and tracts, in letters to the press, and in discussion in the two esoteric journals cited above, accounts were printed which claimed to represent the authentic experience of soldiers in the battle. Some very notable divines, and senior military officers, were amongst those prepared to put their reputation behind these accounts.

The 'factual' versions of the Mons miracles sometimes differ markedly from Machen's story. Three main motifs may be discerned. There is the appearance of St George and/or a phantom army, more usually cavalry than archers; a strange 'cloud' interposing between the British and the enemy and halting the latter's advance; and angels or other heavenly visitants, including one Christlike figure who tends the wounded. The great majority of these accounts have obvious weaknesses: they are second-hand or more often third-hand, they lack names and dates and localities, and they are suspiciously close to the pattern, if not the exact content, of Machen's tale.

Nevertheless, the 'cult' of the 'Angels of Mons', as they had begun indiscriminately to be called, rolled on apace throughout 1915 and generated a literature of its own. Ralph Shirley, the editor of the *Occult Review* and an acquaintance of Machen's, was first among the more responsible accounts, with *Angel Warriors at Mons*, while R. Thurston Hopkins (*War and the Weird*, with A.F. Phillips) and Harold Begbie (*On the Side of the Angels*) were among several of the more credulous chroniclers. A nurse, Phyllis Campbell, contributed to the *Occult Review* and published a book of her own (*Back of the Front*) giving rather florid accounts of her conversations with soldiers at Mons. Machen much later said that he regarded her as one of the 'conscious liars' in the whole affair.

Machen's newspaper, as may be imagined, was keen to make the most of its central role in the story, and gave him space to defend his assertion that 'The Bowmen' was his own invention, and not the recollection of a story he had heard from the front, which was what most supporters of the literal Angels argued. The more indulgent were prepared to concede that Machen may have unconsciously used some hints of actual visions he had heard about and then forgotten. This Machen always absolutely and adamantly denied. Thus, in June 1915, Machen wrote an article refuting a variation on the Angels theme given in a sermon by Dr Horton, a well-known Congregationalist minister (that alone would have been enough to irk Machen); in July he wrote an article 'No Escape from "The Bowmen": My Sympathy with Frankenstein'; in August he replied to Phyllis Campbell's accounts, and in September to Begbie's book; while occasional pieces on the theme continued to appear in 1916 and 1917.

'The Bowmen' was not the only war fantasy Machen had written in 1914. A month later the newspaper also published his 'The Soldier's Rest' which he greatly preferred, and he was encouraged to provide more such fare when the 'Angels' furore was at its height and beyond — *The Great Return* and *The Terror* both owe their origins to the success of 'The Bowmen'.

Three of these other fantasies, together with 'The Bowmen', were collected in a card-covered pocketbook, *The Bowmen — And Other Legends of the War*, published in August 1915. Machen wrote a patient and cogent introduction and postscript, while his friend, the anti-quarian Oswald Barron, who wrote 'The Londoner' column for the paper, contributed an essay facetiously enquiring why other great soldiers and armies — Marlborough, Wellington, Henry Hotspur, Greece, Rome — had not joined in the fray. There was a rapid second edition with two extra stories Machen had meanwhile contributed to the *Evening News*. Machen traces, in his introduction, how the one word 'shining' in his story may have led to the transposition of 'angels' for 'bowmen' and summarizes a typical 'true version' of the story thus: 'Someone (unknown) has met a nurse (unnamed) who has talked to a soldier (anonymous) who has seen angels. But THAT is not evidence; and not even Sam Weller at his gayest would have dared to offer it as such in the Court of Common Pleas'.

What are we to make of this affair at this distance of time? Kevin McClure (*Visions of Bowmen and Angels*, 1993) has conducted a careful review of the contemporary claims made for the Angels and quotes a very level-headed investigation carried out by the Society for Psychical Research, whose report was published in December 1915. It concluded that many of the stories of visions on the battlefield were founded on mere rumour, no first-hand testimony was obtainable and detailed evidence was lacking: but there may be 'a small residue of evidence' to indicate that some men at Mons did 'honestly believe themselves to have had at that time supernormal experience...'.

The best evidence for the existence of strange visions at Mons independent of Machen's story would be first-hand accounts actu-ally predating the publication of the story in the *Evening News* (29 Sept 1914). The nearest approximation to this appears to be the letter sent home by Brigadier-General John Charteris, dated 5 September 1914 in his *At GHQ* (1931) and cited by McClure at the outset of his study: 'Then there is the story of the "Angels of Mons" going strong through the 2nd Corps of how the angel of the Lord on the traditional white horse, and clad all in white with flaming sword, faced the advancing Germans at Mons and forbade their further progress. Men's nerves and imagination play weird pranks in these strenuous times'. The late publication date for this testimony, even though McClure notes there is 'certainly no hint of rewriting or later addi-tion', is not helpful. Even if we conclude that some soldiers, in extreme conditions, may have thought they saw extraordinary things on the battlefield — and hard evidence of even that is dis-tinctly lacking — yet no one can deny it was Machen's story that gave resonance and power to an image, an assurance, that many people in Britain wanted to believe in: the great military tradition characterised by the bowmen of Crecy and Agincourt, and the divine mission of the nation symbolised by the special favour of St George. Machen knew how to invoke ancient symbols to stir the soul — he had already made potent use of the Holy Grail — and we should not let the deceptive slightness of his story, nor all the subsequent anecdotage, distract us from recognising a rare achievement of the imagination.

Nevertheless, Machen was painfully conscious of the irony that this most minor of his stories should find him fame where the arduous craft of his novels and romances had failed. As Purefoy noted, 'People would madden me by asking, "Aren't you proud of your husband?" I used to reply in a snappy way, "I was proud of him long before he wrote 'The Bowmen' ... Have you ever read *The Hill of Dreams?*"' (PM 73 1991). We need have little doubt that few of those who marvelled at 'The Bowmen' had read his earlier work.

Of the other 'legends of the war' written by Machen, 'The Soldier's Rest' comes nearest to achieving the luminosity of 'The Bowmen'. A valorous common soldier finds himself in a rich hospice and is puzzled by the raiment of those who come to praise him, some in picturesque English, and some in strange tongues. We soon surmise what the soldier, at first, does not: he has entered Valhalla. The story concludes with a vision of St Michael, the leader of the Hosts of Heaven, in refulgent armour. 'The Monstrance', detailing the doom that descends on a German sergeant-major guilty of an (unlikely) atrocity, and 'The Dazzling Light', in which an English subaltern has a premonition of later troop movements, are routine by comparison while 'The Little Nations' and 'The Men from Troy', though they broaden the theme a little, are of no great consequence.

Another story which belongs to this period, though it was not published until 1920, has however proved to be rather more enduring than the others. 'The Happy Children' stems from an assignment Machen was given by the *Evening News* in November 1916, which took him to Whitby, the Yorkshire whaling port which Bram Stoker chose as the scene of the arrival of the ship bearing Dracula to England. Machen gave *Evening News* readers an evocative portrait of the old town at night, with its great clifftop abbey, and contributed a second article telling of the town's trade in jet, and the wartime revival of demand for the mourning jewellery made of the black mineral.

ARTHUR MACHEN

In the story, a journalist staying in the ancient harbour town (renamed 'Banwick') goes out for a walk at night — so described that a modern visitor can retrace his steps easily — and sees a procession of wounded children singing and dancing as they ascend the great flight of stone steps up to the Abbey church. Machen's evocation of Whitby is splendid: 'I saw there many gabled houses, sunken with age far beneath the level of the pavement, with dipping roof-trees and bowed doorways, with traces of grotesque carving on their walls. And when I stood on the quay, there on the other side of the harbour was the most amazing confusion of red-tiled roofs that I have ever seen, and the great grey Norman church high on the bare hill above them; and below them the boats swinging in the swaying tide, and the water burning in the fires of the sunset'.

The authentic setting of the story lends it a lustre which some of the other 'legends of the war' lack. The winding white parade of children, its innocent victims proudly displaying their gashes as they cavort beneath the moon, is eerily effective, with a sinister as well as sacred quality about it: while the wartime message (some of the victims are from the *Lusitania*, torpedoed by the Germans) is understated.

While the Angels of Mons furore was just gathering pace, Machen started a series of articles in the newspaper which received much less attention. He had for some time wanted to record his memories of childhood and youth in Gwent and London, and, without knowing of this secret ambition, the paper's editor urged him to do exactly that. As the 'Confessions of a Literary Man', the memoir appeared in thirty-five episodes from March to July 1915, occasionally interrupted, presumably by other demands for space. Each instalment was given a separate heading, from 'In the Days of My Youth' to 'I Translate the *Heptameron* and Disappear'. Martin Secker published the whole set as a single work, *Far Off Things* (without the headings) in 1922, but the original newspaper appearance is still evident in the format of the writing, which is a sequence of passages, each usually starting with some recapitulation of a previous theme, then dwelling upon a new subject, with some digressions here and there, and then working up to its own culmination, often stressing the transitoriness of what has been described.

Thus baldly stated, the book may seem like a journalistic patchwork: but that is far from the case. The episodic structure is not in the least distracting, and may well pass unnoticed by a reader

104

unacquainted with the book's origins. And Machen's prose is at his finest as he evokes a lost golden age in which life was simpler, people were kinder and prouder and the very land, whether in winter or summer, was a great revelation of beauty and wonder. Romanticism, certainly — and some may find it tips over into sentimentality at times — but written with an ardent conviction and directness that makes the reader believe in, or at least want to believe in, what is described. We are enabled to share in the experience of a way of life that has passed entirely; burningly vivid in all its colours and full of character.

For an understanding of Machen's feelings towards his homeland of Gwent, *Far Off Things* is indispensable, recalling the long rambles 'in a very maze of unknown brooks and hills and woods and wild lands' which were the constant recreation of his solitary youth; mourning the passing of the armigerous families of the domain, with their white-walled manors, and the ancient names he borrowed for the squires and mystics of his books — Meyrick and Perrott and Morgan; evoking over and over the great sacred places of the region, Wentwood and Mynydd Maen and the waterpools of the Usk and the surges of the Soar, and circles of druid stones, and holy wells, and wild groves; and reliving his longing to capture the awe and mystery of these places, in such words as he could.

Nor does Machen miss the opportunity to hold forth on his strongly felt beliefs. Here and there the ponderous satire of *Dr Stiggins* is deployed again, but we also have some resumption of the more engaging arguments of *Hieroglyphics*: 'I firmly hold the doctrine that the natural, the arch-natural expression of man, so far as he is to be distinguished from pigs and dogs and goats, is in the arts, and through the arts and by the arts ... once we set aside the "does it pay" nonsense, which is evidently nonsense and pestilent nonsense at that, we come clearly and freely to the truth that man is concerned with beauty, and with the ecstasy or rapture that proceeds from the creation of beauty and from the contemplation of it'. No more forthright defence of the aesthetical standpoint identified with the 'men of the nineties' could be expected, and yet for Machen, the cult of artificially exquisite and precious things is a mean and narrow version of the quest for beauty. He cites instead a Northumbrian serving-maid's lilting local accent as she offered tea one afternoon in a dingy lodging-house for actors: 'her phrase about our tea was chanted to an exquisite melody that might have come from the

Gradual — or from fairyland'.

The latter part of *Far Off Things* takes us to London, and the desolate and austere days Machen spent trying to get literary work of any kind, and he tells it all with a sort of macabre relish, which some may find a mere mask for self-pity. D.H. Lawrence asked, in a letter to their mutual publisher, Martin Secker, 'Why does Machen pity himself so much?' (*The Letters of D.H. Lawrence*, Volume V, Cambridge University Press, 1989, 79). But it is really, I think, an attempt not to inflict too much on the reader of the misery of those days, along with a disinclination on Machen's part to revisit them too closely. Nevertheless, we are left in no doubt as to his extreme relief when he is called back to Gwent: 'I was come to the territory of Caerleon-on-Usk which was Avalon; and every herb of the fields and all the leaves of the wood, and the waters of all the wells and streams were appointed for my healing' he recalls, in pseudo-Biblical language.

Far Off Things is regarded, rightly, as amongst Machen's best successes. D.P.M. Michael dwells upon its gentle qualities, a 'melodious narrative' and 'whimsical spirit', deeming it more reverie than autobiography (DPM 50-51 1971): and this certainly captures one aspect of the book, which has helped to bring Machen a general literary readership distinct from those who came to him for his supernatural horror stories. Morchard Bishop's comparison with De Quincey's *Confessions of an English Opium-Eater* is just. We may even see parallels with the seventeenth century prose of Thomas Traherne, the Herefordshire parson whose *Centuries of Meditation* was not published until 1908, and which is aflame with the same rapture as Machen's evocations of his Gwent childhood:

> The corn was Orient and Immortal Wheat, which never should be reaped, nor was ever sown. I thought it had stood from everlasting to everlasting. The Dust and Stones of the Street were as precious as GOLD: the Gates were at first the End of the World. The Green Trees when I saw them first through one of the Gates transported and Ravished me, their sweetness and unusual Beauty made my Heart to leap, and almost mad with ecstasy, they were such strange and Wonderful Things.

Allowing for the difference in diction across the ages, the exultation and wonder of this piece is as one with the early chapters of *Far Off Things*, and it is remarkable that two such works should arise from the same corner of the country.

The poet Dylan Thomas knew Machen's memoir sufficiently to borrow a phrase from it, unacknowledged, for use in his *Under Milk Wood* (1954). In Chapter one, Machen describes an ancient burial mound, Twyn Barlwm, as 'that mystic tumulus, the memorial of peoples that dwelt in that region before the Celts left the land of Summer', and Thomas gives these words to the Reverend Eli Jenkins in his drama, speaking of Llareggub Hill. Indeed, this character, with his white 'Bardic' hair and sonorous chanting of sacred Welsh place names, may have been partly intended as a spoof on Machen's atavism and Romanticism.

One of the more surprising outcomes of Machen's work for the *Evening News* was a renewed acquaintance with the Anglo-Irish novelist George Moore (1852-1933) who had made a name for himself in the last years of Victoria's reign with grimly realist novels inspired by Zola, including *A Modern Lover* (1883), *A Mummer's Wife* (1885) and *Esther Waters* (1894). Later he had fallen under the influence of Yeats and 'A.E.' and became a staunch proponent of the Celtic in literature, but by 1911 he had become disillusioned with Ireland and began a series of memoirs, such as his autobiographical trilogy *Hail and Farewell* (1911-14) which are amongst the most highly regarded in this form.

Machen had met Moore at the Order of the Golden Dawn early in the century, when he was introduced by Yeats: 'They gave, as it were, a stool to George to sit on; and he was to be a good boy and listen heedfully' Machen recalled in a letter of 1933 (SL 136 1988), aptly capturing the sorcerer's apprentice role Moore initially assumed with Yeats. In his article on acting in *Vanity Fair* (1907), Machen damns *A Mummer's Wife* with faint praise as 'an excellent transcript of life in a ... touring company' but only 'quite a good story as far as it goes': however, he calls Moore's announcement of abandoning English to write in Irish (in the first flush of his newfound Celtism) the talk of a 'rotter' and applies the same term to Moore for his latest book (probably *Memoirs of My Dead Life*, 1906), which Machen terms 'a sort of pocket Casanova'. In a later essay ('The Ready Reporter', 1930) Machen is kinder, remarking without irony that he was glad Moore reconsidered his resolve to write in Irish.

This earlier skirmish does not seem to have prevented the writers striking up a cordial relationship when Machen interviewed Moore for the *Evening News*. During this period he 'saw a great deal of

Moore'. In fact, he wrote features about him on six occasions, one suspects more because they knew each other than because the editor ordered it. Machen acknowledged in a letter of 1931 to his friend, the musician Paul England, 'Moore can write very beautiful and delicate English' but added that his follies and peccadilloes continually spoil the work (SL 228 1988). Moore, for his part, told Machen: 'I've been reading your *Great God Pan*. I didn't make much of it. Confused, it seemed to me. But when I read the Introduction, I said to myself; "Good heavens! Here's a man who writes as well as I do!".' (TNF Chapter eight 1923). Machen added this was 'meant as a very great compliment; indeed so it was' and we may take this remark at face value as evidence that both writers did indeed have a selective regard for each other's work.

Machen's newfound notoriety as a result of the Angels of Mons myths led directly to three more books, all credited as by 'Arthur Machen, Author of "The Bowmen"', and all originally written for and serialised in the *Evening News*. We have already discussed his Grail fantasy *The Great Return* in Chapter five: this appeared in the newspaper just two months after the collection of war legends entitled 'The Bowmen' had been published. But Machen's next book, *The Terror*, which was serialised a year later (October 1916) as 'The Great Terror' and published by Duckworth in February 1917 under the briefer title, was something of a departure for Machen.

True, it was another 'legend of the war': it recounts the rumours and speculation surrounding a series of mysterious deaths in many parts of the country, news of which the authorities suppress. Using the pretext of anti-invasion and anti-espionage precautions, they seal off the localities where the deaths occur, placing sentries to prevent public access. Those who do talk about the incidents can only do so circumspectly, and only a country doctor who has seen some of the victims, and the narrator journalist (Machen as himself again) who has a curiosity about out-of-the-way enigmas can finally piece together the truth: others are reduced to supposing there is a massive, well-planned conspiracy of German infiltrators, or some new weapon unknown to the Allies.

But the story is outside Machen's usual sphere in that any possible supernatural explanation is kept far in the background. All that the reader witnesses is a sequence of inexplicable deaths, and, as in any good murder or suspense thriller, the pleasure is in trying to piece together the clues the author gives, and to arrive at the solution before it is provided at the end. Michael (DPM 49 1971) thinks that the modern reader will solve the case very early on in the book, and hence it will lose much of its interest: but I think this may be the assumption of a Machen scholar, not the general reader. Certainly, I know of new readers of the book who did not guess the solution and were impressed by Machen's skill at supplying reasonable hints while managing not to give the game away. And few would disagree that the suspense, the accumulation of shocking deaths without any clear cause or motivation, is expertly handled.

Savants of Machen's stories of supernatural terror and awe are apt to find *The Terror* unsatisfying: but neither will it entirely please mystery enthusiasts, who may regard the explanation for the killings as a cheat. For they have all been perpetrated by animals: flocks of moths masked and suffocated some victims, cattle gouged or crushed others, even sheep drove cliffwalkers to their deaths. This would be clever as the denouement to a single crime, but in supplying the reason for this revolt of the animals, Machen does not convince, even within the conventions of a mystery yarn. He suggests the creatures may have been infected by the contagion of hatred which is all abroad amongst mankind because of the War: but he rejects this, and proposes instead that the beasts have risen up because they sense a decline in humanity's spiritual ascendancy over them. As the conclusion to what Machen himself dubbed a 'shilling shocker', this seems too ponderous and sounds unconvincing.

Critics are sharply divided about *The Terror*. Reynolds and Charlton call it 'clumsy and long-winded' (RC 119 1963), Michael thinks it is 'rather too laboured' (DPM 49 1971), while Joshi simply says it is 'quite bad' (SJ 31 1990). But Paul Jordan-Smith thought it 'far more exciting than ... Conan Doyle' and superior to Poe (PJS 227 1923), and Wesley Sweetser numbers it amongst Machen's masterpieces, as 'one of the most striking proofs of Machen's originality in the fabrication of ideas' (WS 128 1964). Certainly it proved one of the more popular of his works, with a new and revised edition in Duckworth's flagship 'New Readers Library' and inclusion in Edward Wagenknecht's anthology for the American 'Viking Portable Library', *Six Novels of the Supernatural*. Some have also pointed to the possible influence of the theme on Daphne du Maurier's story 'The Birds', and therefore of course on Alfred Hitchcock's famed film of the same title, but there is no direct evidence that this was inspired by Machen's plot.

A judicious summary of the book would acknowledge its success as a superior suspense thriller while conceding that, once the secret is out, there is considerably less motivation to reread the book: whereas usually the pervasive otherworldliness of Machen's work lures the reader back frequently. Nevertheless, Machen's sure hand at evoking lonely and wild countryside is often in evidence — the setting is once again principally the Pembrokeshire coast around Tenby, with several lightly-disguised locations — and the novel has also some interest, indirectly, as a depiction of the fevered atmosphere of the war years. That the state should exercise such totalitarian censorship and suppression was fiction, but a fiction that Machen's readers could accept as credible and within their own experience.

The third book billed as 'by the author of "The Bowmen"', was *War and the Christian Faith*, a brief sixty-four page reprint of articles Machen had contributed to the *Evening News* under the title 'God and the War', in 1917: Machen did not think much of the publisher's retitling of his work. An earlier essay on the theme had been sub-titled, 'To Those Whose Faith is Sorely Tried', and this reflects Machen's main purpose. He did not expect the book to be a success, and the 'Bowmen' by-line may by now have been losing its efficacy, for it did not prevent him from being proved right. As with *The Great Return* the public did not seem ready for spiritual literature which looked at more profound themes than the patriotic talismans of the 'legends of the war'.

After the war, Machen found his newspaper employment more and more intolerable and his work receiving less appreciation. He recalls in *Things Near and Far*, his second volume of autobiography, how the paper's proprietor, Lord Northcliffe, dismissed an article in which he took great pride (it compared the individuality of cottages with the repetition of modern city streets, and used this contrast to argue that strangeness is necessary to the highest beauty) 'with venom as a "wiseacre article"' in one of his circulars to staff. Recalling his employers from the 1880s, he notes ruefully: 'after more recent experiences of mine I am very loath to find fault with any persons who treat those in their employment as human beings, with the decent civilities, courtesies and considerations that are befitting between man and man. In those days I had no knowledge of the anthropoids'. He gained his freedom from the paper when he wrote a forthright obituary notice of Lord Alfred Douglas. Unfortunately, the litigious peer had not in fact died, and Machen was made a scapegoat for the resultant libel action. He left the paper in November 1921.

Seven: The World Beyond

Shortly after he left the *Evening News*, interest in Machen's work began to increase considerably, both in Britain and America, so that by 1923 he was for a while established as something like a 'Grand Old Man of Letters'. In that year Martin Secker published all his major works in uniform volumes, the Caerleon Edition; Henry Danielson published a bibliography, with commentary by Machen; there were features in several periodicals; an exhibition of his books was held in New York; his second volume of autobiography, *Things Near and Far* appeared; and the First Edition Bookshop commissioned and published two elegant opuscules, evidence of his interest for collectors.

It is difficult to identify precisely why this onrush of recognition, denied to him in a literary career of forty years, should suddenly occur. Certainly the Angels of Mons episode, and his fine autobiographical volumes, had kept his name before the public, and had perhaps thrown off the association with the macabre, which may have limited the appeal of his earlier works. Also, the temper of the times may have been favourable: Machen could be appreciated by both the pastoral and lyrical Georgian coterie, and those Roaring Twenties diehards ready to find common ground with artists previously shunned.

The impetus for the American enthusiasm for his work started with Chicago newspaperman Vincent Starrett, whose *Arthur Machen, Novelist of Ecstasy and Sin* — the first critical study of Machen — was published in 1918. Emphasising, perhaps rather unduly, Machen's interest in paganism, Starrett painted readers an alluring picture: 'He writes of the life Satyr-ic. For him Pan is not dead; his votaries still whirl through woodland windings to the mad pipe that was Syrinx, and carouse fiercely in enchanted forest grottoes'; while lauding his prose style equally ardently ('his sentences move to sonorous, half-submerged rhythms, swooning with pagan colour and redolent of sacerdotal incense'). Starrett ends with a clarion call: 'posterity is going to demand of us why, when the opportunity was ours, we did not open our hearts to Arthur Machen and name him among the very great'. With Machen's permission, Starrett also collected two volumes of essays, fragments and old stories, *The Shining Pyramid* (Chicago, 1923) and *The Glorious Mystery* (Chicago, 1924). These led to an unpleasant episode. The American demand for Machen's work, which Starrett had inspired, resulted in the established New York publisher Alfred A. Knopf acquiring the rights in the U.S.A. for virtually all Machen's work. Machen had forgotten remarks made in earlier letters to Starrett, giving him a free hand to promote and publish his work, and joined with Knopf in accusing Starrett of issuing the two collections piratically. The two men settled their differences openly and cordially when Starrett visited Machen in London, but the episode could not wholly be forgotten and, as late as 1977, Starrett's literary executor Michael Murphy arranged issue of the full facts and correspondence to set the matter straight (*Starrett vs. Machen*, St Louis, Missouri, 1977).

Other American literary figures who fervently proclaimed Machen's work included James Branch Cabell, the author of *Jurgen*, who praised him in his bookish fantasy *Beyond Life* (1919), Robert Hillyer, Professor of English at Harvard; the dandy and aesthete Carl Van Vechten, who included a purple passage proclaiming the master in his novel *Peter Whiffle* (1922); and Californian don Paul Jordan-Smith, who eulogised Machen in his *On Strange Altars* (1923). The first thesis on Machen was also supplied by an American, Ralph Grainger Morrissey, in 1930.

The British interest was by comparison modest, and tended to treat Machen as a 'character' rather than the magus envisioned by the American proselytes: his Johnsonian appearance and oratory, his sartorial eccentricity and his conviviality are celebrated rather more than his writing. Nevertheless it must have been pleasing to Machen, so long used to regarding reviews with a kind of gallows humour, to find a reviewer of *Far Off Things* opening with the remark, 'Mr Arthur Machen is now, at long last, acknowledged to be one of the most arresting and distinguished writers of our time' (S.M. Ellis, *The Fortnightly Review*, January 1923); or a feature which states 'incidentally', as if it were an accepted fact, 'all the author's work ... is a masterpiece of beautiful prose' (Geoffrey H. Wells, in *Cassell's*

Weekly, October 1923).

These were halcyon days indeed for Machen. Since 1919 he and Purefoy had lived at a most hospitable house, hard by Regent's Park. The house, 12 Melina Place, St John's Wood, with its wild garden, was the haven the Machens had long looked for, and especially a boon now that there were two children in the family, Hilary (born 1912) and Janet (1917). Machen was to immortalise the house by making its garden the scene of a splendid spoof, of which more later. But 12 Melina Place also lived long in the memory of the rest of his family. Purefoy looked upon it as the first real home she had known since childhood and recalled many details of it with fondness:

> The first morning I woke, it was wintry weather. I saw the huge old pear-tree, which nearly touched my bedroom window, covered with blossom and snow. How I learnt to love that tree! I think it looked most beautiful in full bloom, on a moonlight night ... The house was not really old, only about a hundred years, I should think, but it had the look of age, and the rooms, though small, were well proportioned, with snug low ceilings.
> (PM 82-3 1991)

For Hilary Machen, writing over forty years later, the pleasant memories of those days were still fresh in the mind. The house was:

> everything that a house should be, except for the kitchen range, which moved my mother, and Elsie, the *bonne*, to antiphonal strong language. In the front was a room lined with books, and against the only bare wall was a Broadwood piano, another mark of prosperity ... My mother was a pianist of parts, fiery and inaccurate, and she played Bach organ Fugues and sometimes stopped with a hearty 'Damn' at a missed pedal entry: at which Arthur would look up from Copperfield or Quixote and say, mildly, 'Why don't you dash away like Burney?' to which my mother would reply, heartily, 'Old Idiot!' and Arthur would chuckle, and twist his feet together ...
> There was a dining room behind, with a desk and many more books, where my mother served rare and delicious meals, and where my father sat down to write in the evenings, with a muttered lamentation, 'Mutton chops, mutton chops'. So that even now I see the curse of Adam in that joint.
> Overhead were three small bedrooms and an oak-pan-

elled bathroom: and nearly all the windows, above and below, looked out into the garden in which my mother showed as much skill and success as she did in the kitchen; and behind, to corners of other small houses, hidden among the fruit trees, which were the survivors of the eighteenth century market-gardening wood.

('In My Father's House', *The Aylesford Review*, Spring 1963)

The novelist Anthony Powell recalled in a review also forty years later how Machen had come to his notice: 'When I was a boy I used sometimes to catch a glimpse of Arthur Machen in St John's Wood, with his longish white hair and Inverness cape, every inch a nineteenth century literary man ... one sees that was exactly what he was, a type, I think it would be true to say, now entirely extinct. It is impossible to imagine anyone these days having the career Machen had'. Powell added, 'he seems always to have been able to extract a good deal of enjoyment out of life' (*Under Review*, Heinemann, 1991: originally *Daily Telegraph*, 1963).

Machen's role as man-of-letters and his gusto for good company were indeed amply demonstrated at Melina Place. As his literary fame grew, the house became a shrine for admirers, including many from America, who, along with old friends from the stage, the tavern and the press, were served with a devilish punch of Machen's own devising.

Hilary recalled, 'After dinner, before the first ring at the bell, my father and I got out the ingredients for the punch: a two gallon earthenware jar, Gin, Burgundy and Sauterne, in due and large proportion, bottles of the stuff; and the glasses were large, thick and bell-shaped'. The soirées held at Melina Place seem to have been an even more boisterous and bohemian version of the Gray's Inn gatherings twenty years before, and they were far from purely literary. Amongst those who attended were Augustus John, with his entourage of fair maidens, the composer John Ireland, Roald Amundsen the explorer, publisher Peter Davies, old friends such as Jerome and Jepson, humorist D.B. Wyndham Lewis, society novelist Elinor Wylie, Irish author Norah Hoult, and J.C. Squire, editor of *The London Mercury* and leading Georgian poet and critic, as well as numerous Bensonians, and a seasoning of occultists and theosophists.

But while Machen's newly acclaimed status enabled him to find an outlet for old, obscure and ephemeral work, and brought back most of his books to print, he found it difficult to supply new writing. His days at the *Evening News* had harried him to the extent that his health and equilibrium had suffered, and had made him reluctant to write anything without a clear commission. Despite some reservations about Martin Secker (he called him a 'rogue', which was quite mild compared with his views on Grant Richards) he agreed to provide a continuation of *Far Off Things*, and finished this by August 1922, telling Starrett he was 'a little weary of it', it was 'beneath the level of *Far Off Things*' but not, he hoped, 'devoid of interest'.

The first volume of autobiography had ended, as it began, with Machen in his early twenties translating *The Heptameron* in his father's rectory at Llanddewi. The sequel starts with a poignant recreation of his father's return from Oxford to Caerleon, meeting his sisters on 'the old dim yellow and faded chocolate omnibus from the Bull' and exchanging talk of the college and the little Gwent town. It is expertly depicted, so that in a few paragraphs we feel we know the characters, as in a Dickens novel. And then Machen snatches it all away: 'Alas! They are all dead, years and years ago ... And those of the party that lived longer knew more of sorrow, and more of broken hopes and of dreams that never came true': and he warns us that he has started thus 'advisedly', for he too has known the same disappointments. This does indeed set the tone for *Things Near and Far*, which does not revisit Gwent very much more, and so loses the illumination of Machen's prose which always occurs when he talks of his country.

Machen was right. The second volume does not sustain the high standard he had set with *Far Off Things*. It is more diffuse, with some long asides that do not contribute anything to his story; and it is also more bitter. Machen had hidden some of the hardships he endured in his early years under a protective persiflage, but in *Things Near and Far* he is more inclined to grouch. Nevertheless, the book has 'interest', to use Machen's modest term, in particular for chapters nine and ten in which he recounts the strange experiences that seemed to cluster around his life at the turn of the century. His account of days on the stage is full of mild good humour and camaraderie, causing regret that he did not write a full length recollection of his acting career, which might have enjoyed the affection later given to J.B. Priestley's *The Good Companions*. *Things Near and Far* concludes briskly, with a refusal to say anything of his journalistic career at all.

In the twenties and thirties, several collections of Machen's essays appeared. The first two were the finest. *Strange Roads* and *With the Gods in Spring* (1923) was a brief pocket-book, pleasantly illustrated, containing two rural idylls that had originally appeared in the journal *Out and Away* a few years earlier. They are exquisite encapsulations of twin Machen themes; the ageless wonder of nature, and the journey as a search for some meaning we cannot quite catch. Strongly and oratorically expressed, there is an abiding majesty but also a resonant simplicity in Machen's words:

> We shall go on seeking it to the end, so long as there are men on earth. We shall seek it in all manner of strange ways; some of them wise, and some of them unutterably foolish. But the search will never end. It is the secret of things; the real truth that is everywhere hidden under outward appearances. There are many ways of the great quest of the secret.

This chapbook was followed in 1924 by a more substantial collection, *Dog and Duck*. In elegant blue alligatored boards and a limited edition of nine hundred from a young and tasteful publisher, Jonathan Cape, this was one of the books which gave Machen greatest pleasure. Subtitled, 'A London Calender Et Cetera', the calendrical element is a learned but light-hearted sequence of meditations on festivals and seasons, such as 'The Merry Month of May', 'Martinmas', 'Where are the Fogs of Yesteryear'. The title essay, however, is a splendid spoof which purports to revive interest in an old bowling game involving an elaborate courtyard. Passing allusions to the game, anciently known as Chase Mallard, are quoted from historical sources as diverse as a Chaucerian poet and a Regency murder trial. But all of this is a pleasant hoax, for the game was played only within living memory in Machen's time, and only in one place, namely, the garden at his home in Melina Place.

The same year saw a collection of contributions to *The Academy* gathered with some stories in an American edition only as *The Glorious Mystery*. In 1926, two anthologies appeared: *Dreads and Drolls* was drawn from Machen's contributions to *The London Graphic* in the previous year, and deals with historical mysteries, London byways and the old days and old ways, while *Notes and Queries* is a revival of articles from *T.P's Weekly* (1908-9). Neither of these collections have quite the same coherence or mellow assurance as *Dog and*

Duck, they have about them more of the flavour of work to order. Two later volumes, *The Glitter of the Brook* (1932) and *Bridles and Spurs* (1951) were issued by small presses in the USA only. Many more of Machen's essays remain for rediscovery and reprinting and these will always be greeted with enthusiasm by admirers of his prose style: they could also find appreciation amongst lovers of tradition.

Joshi (SJ 18 1990) sees Machen's essays as a diversion from his true work written with 'an evil facility ... Machen no longer wrote about anything, he wrote around it. A style that had once been the jewelled distillation of anguish becomes the desultory meanderings of a man who has grown too fond of his own literary voice'; the essays are 'too discursive to merit real greatness; they never deliver the substance their themes seem to promise'.

It is hard to criticise a writer for continuing to write, especially when they have to do so for a livelihood. Joshi is judging Machen by austere literary canons, but it is not clear whether he has considered Machen's work in the context of the classical English essay, the form mastered by Charles Lamb, William Hazlitt or Thomas de Quincey. In their work, which was certainly very familiar and fond to Machen, discursiveness is part of the essence of the essay, and style must seek grace, and a certain mock-gravity rather than burning zeal. As Reynolds and Charlton observe, 'Elegant table-talk of a literary and personal kind is not much regarded today ... But to the essay lover he has much to offer ...' (RC 136 1963).

Sweetser, too, has praise for the wit and charm of *Dog and Duck* and what he calls its 'Machenisms', 'a pet theory or satirical reference'. Instead of being desultory, Sweetser sees the essays as taking a definite stance in favour of traditionalism and old-fashioned qualities, the love of customs and courtesy.

In the same vein as his essays, and with the same unique savour, is one of his most curious books, *The London Adventure*. This was a commission from Martin Secker, who found some success in reprinting Machen's major work in slim green 7s 6d volumes as part of his New Adelphi Library series, in company with titles by D.H. Lawrence, Norman Douglas and other authors not quite in the mainstream of the public's literary appreciation. The book has been described as a third volume of autobiography, and indeed Machen does tell us something of his days as a newspaper man: the opening chapter has a particularly bitter denunciation of the indignities of wage labour, showing that his experiences at the *Evening News* still rankled after the passing of several years: 'Hence, I say, my profound contempt for all those who praise "work" and the ways of honest living, which are mostly degradations somewhat below those experienced by the procurer of Soho. Hence, my profound gratitude for the bliss of idleness ...'.

But drawing upon his own experiences do not make *The London Adventure* a memoir, nor was it intended as such. Machen tells us of the genesis of the book in an amusing fashion in the opening chapter when his publisher seeks him out at an obscure inn and reminds him of his promise 'to write a book about London ... a really great book ... of ... unknown, unvisited squares in Islington, dreary byways in Holloway ... arches and viaducts in the region of Camden Town'. This celebration of the uncelebrated London we do, in some measure, get in the book, yet only in odd diversions: it does not make up the prevailing theme.

Both Reynolds and Charlton and D.P.M. Michael see *The London Adventure* as an attempt again at the theme of *A Fragment of Life*, the presence of the outré in the outwardly ordinary, the finding of strangeness and splendour in the dingiest and drabbest places: but both conclude it is a failed attempt. Joshi succinctly summarises the exasperation, and perhaps the grudging admiration, some readers will feel: '... the whole London Adventure is about Machen's not having written a book called *The London Adventure*'. Machen himself was a hard critic of the book: 'It is very bad; and very sad for me. You in your day will find out the misery of failing or failed powers' (letter to Colin Summerford, August 1924).

Yet this distress at his inability to write the book he intended does not show in the book he did write, where it is instead the subject of banter and a certain complicit game-playing with the reader. We should recall that Machen had evinced despair at the actual achievement of his books as against the image, the vision, ever since *The Anatomy of Tobacco* forty years before.

The London Adventure is best read as an extended personal essay and its rambling among odd incidents, stray notions, and curious theories can be splendidly diverting. It is not a work to inspire the ardour felt for *The Hill of Dreams* or the relish of *The Three Impostors*, but it is vintage Machen and comparable with the work of contemporaries such as Chesterton or Belloc.

By one of those coincidences which Machen himself enjoyed — and to which he makes a brief reference — a book in a very similar red cloth and format, entitled *The London Venture*, appeared at about the same time. This was a reprint of Michael Arlen's first book. He had recently achieved bestseller popularity for his romance *The Green Hat*. His early novel (1921) has some literary similarities to Machen's too, in that it is part autobiography, part meditation upon the bizarre happenstances in London streets, and with the same deceptively languorous, often lazy way of telling. Whether Secker was aware of the parallels and hoped Machen's book might profit thereby is not certain.

'Wandering a little is almost a hobby of mine' says Machen in the third chapter of this book, and indeed the subtitle is 'The Art of Wandering'. Machen is offhand about this characteristic, yet it is a gentle and a generous quality, a sharing of enthusiasms, the quality of the raconteur and the good companion and not lightly to be despised. Machen had made his contribution to the rare and high in literature in his youth: it is understandable that he still hankered for the sublimities of these writings, but the assurance of his style and the breadth of his experience, permeating the whole of *The London Adventure*, make it a quaint and fascinating, a friendly and distinctive read.

In expressing his old theme, Machen nowhere loses his touch for the memorable refrain, the sonorous phrase, for example: 'Strangeness which is the essence of beauty is the essence of truth, and the essence of the world'. Machen would have found an ironic delight in the fact that for a period in the 1970s and 1980s, *The London Adventure*, the book he so lamented, was his only title in print, and for some of that time was chiefly available from a bookseller with the unlikely name of Horace C. Blossom who also diversified as a gentleman's outfitter.

Peter Davies, one of the young habitués of the Melina Place evenings, had begun his own adventure in publishing and in 1925, when he translated the French epicure Anthelme Brillat-Savarin's *Physiologie du goût* (1825), a witty meditation upon the art of the dinner-table, he chose Machen to write the introduction. Machen as gourmet might have seemed incongruous to those whose saw him as a rarefied magus, but in fact he had always possessed a great relish for good food and drink, which he indulged as far as his means would allow. 'England will never be Merry England once more till we return to the Catholic Faith, Beef Steaks (with an onion, if you will), and the Strongest Ale: this last to be consumed in enormous quantities' he had proclaimed in a letter to Edgar Jepson in 1910 (SL 241 1992), and we note the due emphasis put upon the things of the plate and the palate. Machen had once defined the aim of mysticism as 'bringing humanity to exquisite perfection' (*Evening News*, 4 March 1913) and this he thought a principle applicable to daily life too: in his introduction to Brillat-Savarin, he states '... those who aim at perfection aim at perfection in all things. Their desire is for the best: for the best music, and the best drink, and the best meat that are to be had'. But he was careful to distinguish this doctrine from the undiscriminating love of luxury: 'I have had luxurious meals at the Hotel Splendide and the Hotel Glorieux which were costly rubbish. I have lunched on bread, and cheese, and beer to admiration, but then the bread, and cheese, and beer were all the best of their kind: a good Caerphilly cheese is better than a raw, unripe, stinging Stilton; as decent honest beer — if you can get any — is infinitely above third-rate champagne'. And he also makes the point that, no matter how good the food, it will turn to ashes if the company is not also good. Deploring the poor cuisine available in most English eating-houses, Machen concludes his introduction with the hope that this new edition of *The Physiology of Taste* will 'light a fire in the land'. He continued his crusading for true food in a series of articles for the *Sunday Express* in 1928, with such enticing themes as 'The Secret of Roast Fowl', 'Adventures with Cheeses' and, more esoterically, 'Cawl and Marigolds'.

Some publishing commissions, though a welcome source of income, were less congenial. In 1925 he provided for Chatto and Windus an account of a mysterious eighteenth century disappearance, *The Canning Wonder*, and in 1927 he wrote text to accompany illustrations for a book on Fleet Street. But the publisher, Eyre and Spottiswoode, did not think Machen's writing sufficiently compatible and another author was commissioned to provide the published text. During this period also Machen worked as a reader for Ernest Benn publishers, from 1927-1933, work which he found generally tiresome.

The Machen euphoria of the post-war years had begun to fade away somewhat by the late 1920s, though a steadfast group of admirers remained in contact with the author. The focus of this coterie moved in 1929, when the Machens, who had been forced to leave their beloved Melina Place two years earlier, and had made do with a less congenial stop-gap in Loudoun Road, St John's Wood, finally settled in Old Amersham, Buckinghamshire. It may seem curious that Machen did not choose to retire to Gwent, but changes to Caerleon, his home town, especially the building of a red brick asylum and some factories, had marred its beauty for him. He probably also took into account that he would be wise to remain within easy distance of London if he wished to pick up further literary work. The Machens settled well in their modest rooms in Amersham, becoming regular pilgrims to the local inn, the King's Arms, and the parish church: Machen wrote anonymously a pamphlet about the parish, published in 1930. What he thought of the memorial to Protestant martyrs burned on a hill above the town is not recorded.

Their new home in the High Street in Amersham, Lynwood, had been found for them by their niece, Sylvia Townsend Warner, the daughter of Purefoy's eldest sister Norah and a Harrow schoolmaster. Sylvia had been a frequent visitor to Melina Place, and her love of this part of Buckinghamshire had been channelled into her first novel, *Lolly Willowes* (1926). Musical, like her aunt and cousin Hilary, she had co-edited a ten volume study of Tudor church music (1923-29) but was now establishing a reputation as a creative writer too. Her work, comprising seven novels, four volumes of poetry, eight volumes of short stories, a book of essays and a biography of the Arthurian fantasist T.H. White, is currently receiving greater attention, especially her masterpiece, *The Corner That Held Them* (1947).

Though the style is lighter than Machen's, it is difficult not to see in the theme of *Lolly Willowes*, a 'respectable' woman turning to witchcraft to throw off the oppression of the roles expected of her, an echo of several of his stories. We are reminded of the young women in 'The White People', 'The Ceremony' and 'The Turanians' for whom a more vital, pagan way of life is an irresistible call and a great liberation. The heroine's dalliance with the Devil, though it is handled in a subtle and naturalistic way far removed from Machen's purple prose, is bound to recall the theme of *The Great God Pan*. Given the family connection, and the intensified attention Machen's work had received during this period, it is not unreasonable to suppose that his stories influenced the theme of Sylvia's first novel and the significance of the Chiltern countryside was clearly her equivalent of Gwent for Machen.

Sylvia remained close to the Machens in their old age, and on one occasion when they visited her in East Chaldon, on the Dorset coast, she took Arthur to see T.F. Powys, author of *Mr Weston's Good Wine* and other rural fables. Though he was notoriously austere and their views could scarcely have commended themselves to each other, he and Machen got on very well.

Hilary, Machen's son, commented in his unpublished memoirs that while 'technically Sylvia far outstripped him' his father 'was able to reach heights and depths quite beyond Sylvia', adding that she said as much to him a few weeks before she died. It is a judicious comparison, though Machen was not quite so wanting in the technique of fiction, nor Sylvia as modest in her achievements as it suggests.

A street fair held in Old Amersham High Street each September became a favourite event which the Machens commemorated with a boisterous party to which old and new friends flocked. There is a vivid recreation of one such gathering in that curious memoir *Peterley Harvest* by 'David Peterley' (1960) which attests in particular to the lethal and disorienting qualities of the host's punch drink.

Visitors to Amersham included Colin Summerford who had sought out Machen in 1924, when, as a Winchester schoolboy with a precocious interest in Celtic legend, he had been inspired by *The Secret Glory*. He remained a frequent visitor to the last, and was one of the organisers of an appeal fund for Machen. Working on an anthology of Irish literature for Methuen, he made the acquaintance of the Fenian fantasist James Stephens (1882-1950), whose Celtic saga *The Crock of Gold* Machen had favourably reviewed on its publication in 1912. He was able to introduce the two ageing authors in 1945, when Machen found Stephens 'a very rare fellow and fine company' (SL 163 1988).

Summerford also introduced Machen to the poet John Betjeman, another enthusiast of *The Secret Glory*, as we have seen; Betjeman in turn was able to guide to Machen's door *The Observer* film critic C.A. Lejeune and her son Anthony, who has written a moving memoir of Machen in his last years ('An Old Man and a Boy', in *Arthur Machen; Memories and Impressions*, St Albert's Press, Llandeilo, 1960).

Oliver Stonor, later to write novels and literary studies as 'Morchard Bishop', met Machen in 1926, and he and his first wife, the Irish novelist Norah Hoult, were regular visitors. Frank Baker, who had won acclaim for his gentle fantasy *Miss Hargreaves* (1940), about an invented spinster poet who comes to life (played by Margaret

Rutherford in a 1953 stage version), made Machen's acquaintance in 1942. Several of his subsequent novels bear Machen's influence, including *Allanyr* (1942), set in Caerleon, and *Before I Go Hence* (1946), an enigmatic ghost story.

Baker recalled a typical meeting with Machen and Purefoy at the local inn, the King's Arms:

> this exuberant and always jovial pair ... never seemed old; and although with beautiful courtesy they were always able to make us feel we were their contemporaries, they were completely at ease with our own years. In his outward person Arthur presented both the great man of letters and the actor-manager of bygone times: a black topcoat with an ulster cape over his broad shoulders; black wide-brimmed hat; a round and very solid head with brilliant blue eyes, and a tonsure fringed by the silky white hair ... Everyone who knew Machen is agreed that he was one of the last great conversationalists ... And Mr Machen's views were always strong; or, if he had no views, he would lead into an anecdote, the laughter would be fine, another round of drinks would be called for, tobacco relit, and you were ready for the next act ... the tenderness, the all-enfolding gusty humour, the Rabelaisian rumbustiouness which made up the greater part of him very soon came bubbling out.
>
> (FB 222-4 1968)

Machen remained a working writer even though in 'retirement', and soon found a new outlet. The late 1920s saw the mushrooming of anthologies solely devoted to horror and supernatural fiction, typified by the *Not At Night* series edited by Christine Campbell Thomson from 1925 to 1937 (twelve titles), Charles Birkin's *Creeps* series from 1932 to 1936 (fourteen titles) and Dorothy L. Sayers' *Detection, Mystery and Horror* volumes (1929-34, three titles). These did much to speed the process of separating work in this field from the mainstream of literature, so that today Machen is often pigeon-holed as a 'horror writer' as if this were an adequate encapsulation of his work. The anthologies edited by Lady Cynthia Asquith, beginning with *The Ghost Book* in 1926, do not quite fall into this category, for rather than using work by pulp purveyors of the sensational, paid to supply by the yard, she often turned to authors of established literary reputation or those who showed promise of this. *The Ghost Book* includes stories by Hugh Walpole, D.H. Lawrence, L.P. Hartley,

Mary Webb and Clemence Dane, while Machen, Algernon Blackwood and Walter de la Mare, though acknowledged masters of the
eerie, were also respected craftsmen.

Machen made six original contributions to Lady Asquith's collections and they represent his only known new fiction written in the
decade 1921-31. His contribution to *The Ghost Book*, indeed, had
earlier origins, for 'Munitions of War', in which sailors of Nelson's
time are seen helping to load Royal Navy ships during the Great
War, is merely a variation on 'The Bowmen', brief, atmospheric and
effective, but nothing new. Of the remaining pieces, two, 'The
Islington Mystery' (for *The Black Cap*, 1927) and 'The Cosy Room'
(for *Shudders*, 1928), are clever and macabre, but not supernatural,
and represent no more than solid professional work, while two
more, 'Johnny Double' (for *The Treasure Cave*, 1928) and 'Awaking'
(for *The Children's Cargo*, 1930), are intended for children, though the
latter finds Machen excelling in painting a word-picture of a Midsummer Fair whose colours and tumult would probably delight a
child:

> Here was, first of all, the encampment of the Knights, jewelled
> with pavilions of gold and green, of silver and crimson, of
> scarlet and purple; the banners all figured with lions and
> dragons, wyverns and leopards, flying over them; and the
> place prepared for the joust ... Presently, the ringing trumpets
> echoed from the hill and the thunder of the horses' hoofs
> answered, and the two knights in their glittering armour
> clashed together ... There was silken and rich stuff blazing in
> the sunlight; there was a man with a bird of all colours that
> spoke and uttered words and sentences. There were cups of
> gold and silver and vessels of brass; there were puppets that
> went dancing and did a mystery before all; there were swords
> and armour, and jars of wine, and meat roasting, and horns
> calling, and a man that came with a pipe and drum and morris
> men following him, and a fool in gold and green, arm in arm
> with a grisly Death.

Yet Machen snatches all this away: for when he awakes, the boy of
the story finds himself in a grey and dreary world where his tale of
the Fair is disbelieved and he is prescribed as suffering from sun-
stroke. It is, of course, the modern world. We are probably to take
this as a timeslip story or alternative world, and in this it predates
several popular children's novels of twenty and thirty years later, so

that it is tempting to wonder whether Machen could have sufficiently softened his satire and dogmatism to write a full-length children's book.

Machen's final story for a Cynthia Asquith collection is of a different order than the others. 'Opening the Door' (for *When Churchyards Yawn*, 1931) is deceptively simple. The clergyman Secretan Jones, living quietly in a London square, is preoccupied (like the Darnells in *A Fragment of Life*) with mundane matters. He goes out of his garden one evening — and vanishes for six weeks. Yet when he returns, he is convinced he has only been away a little while, and the flower he claims he plucked as he left the garden is still fresh. The narrator, a newspaper reporter (ie, Machen in his *Evening News* days), gains his acquaintance and learns something more of the matter: odd dreams, memory losses and other incidents, trivial enough in themselves, have bothered the clergyman, who is immersed in recondite liturgical study into the lost Rite of the Celtic Church; and the reader perceives that there must be some pattern to these events, if only we can find it. Vestiges of what was revealed to him when he was away from this world begin to seep back into Secretan Jones's consciousness, and he goes away to stay at a farm near Llanthony Abbey, in the Black Mountains, for rest. This time he goes out and does not return.

Machen has resumed a favourite theme — the intermingling of this world and another of far vaster significance — and he succeeds, in a brief space, in quietly and suggestively conveying the sublime and awesome mystery of this otherworld. The reader is left to ponder upon the allusiveness of the story.

A straying into an otherworld is the theme also of 'N', an enigmatic story Machen wrote especially for a collection, *The Cosy Room*, that was otherwise filled with reprints, some of them very minor. The poet and bibliophile John Gawsworth had persuaded publishers Rich and Cowan to issue the book, which was padded out with slight tales Machen had contributed to periodicals almost fifty years earlier. Gawsworth's youth was devoted to championing neglected authors. He made Machen's acquaintance when only seventeen; issued when eighteen (1930) two volumes depicting photographs of *The Residences of Arthur Machen*; wrote a pastiche Machen short story 'Above the River', and got Machen to write a preface for a limited edition of it which they both signed (he was then nineteen); and at twenty edited an anthology, *Strange Assembly* (1932) which included two reprinted Machen tales. He also aspired to write a biography of Machen but although he did much work on this it never found a publisher. The letters between them reveal Machen as grateful for the campaigning zeal of his young disciple, but also slightly embarrassed. He told Colin Summerford, when *The Cosy Room* was about to appear, in Spring 1936, 'There are things in it, dating from 1890, that make me sick to look at. Nevertheless, since (Gawsworth) went through the pains of digging them all out, typing them when dug, finding an agent, getting them published, and getting me some money — I felt forced in mere decency to dedicate the book to him'.

We should be grateful for Gawsworth's persistence, for 'N' is vintage Machen, a story which has all the elusive dimension of 'Opening the Door', but an even greater grace in the telling, harking back to the heightened prose of *The Secret Glory* and *The Great Return*.

True to his belief that the spiritually significant can be found in the most mundane regions, and not only in legend-charged land like his own Gwent, the setting for 'N' is the placid London suburb of Stoke Newington. One of Machen's idle scholar characters pieces together descriptions from various sources of a wonderful garden which can be found in the area, but which it is difficult to locate in the geographical sense. The strayers into this pleasaunce include a decidedly bluff type who thinks only that he found a particularly pleasant park: but also a devout student of the German mystic Boehme and his English disciple William Law; and a young lunatic. The lead character surmises that there is an interpenetration between our own world and another, and there is an implication that not all traffic with the otherworld is without peril.

Connected with 'N' and 'Opening the Door' is another late work by Machen, his last novel, *The Green Round* (1933). Machen did not think highly of this book, which was commissioned by Benn for a series of cheap popular novels, and he confessed he only perservered in writing it because the publisher paid an advance. Even then, the sixty thousand words required was hard going for Machen, and this shows in the writing, where he several times repeats what has already been narrated, without adding anything new. The inner element of the novel has interest because of its dwelling upon the otherworld theme, but Machen may have thought this alone was too mystical for Benn's use, so he returns once more to the Little People to supply drama and horror to his plot.

The protagonist, Hillyer, is a scholarly recluse who finds his mind wandering somewhat and, on doctor's orders, goes for a change of air to Pembrokeshire — the Tenby area again, which takes the place of Gwent. His walks take him to an old earthwork, the 'Green Round' of the title, where he often passes the time. A sudden change of attitude among the other guests at his hotel, who shun and condemn him for no clear reason, forces him back to London, where more strange events occur. We learn more about Hillyer's researches, which concern stories of those who visit fairyland, and parallels with other visions of marvellous realms (we sense Machen emptying his notebooks again). Hillyer discovers a curious book by a Victorian clergyman who meditates upon the transformation of everyday scenes that can be effected at dawn or sunset, and speculates upon more complete transformations such as those sought for by the alchemists. (Machen reuses the clergyman, Reverend Thomas Hampole, and his book, in 'N'). Hillyer ponders 'whether it be lawful to regain or attempt to regain the Earthly Paradise; to pass, as it were, under the guard of the flaming swords; to recover a state which is represented as definitely ended, so far as bodily existence is concerned'. In other words, the seeking after a literal (not metaphorical) 'heaven on earth' could be a heinous sin which imperils the soul of the seeker. And Hillyer does have such a momentary experience, involuntarily as it seems, in which his lodgings are transformed into a palace.

Unfortunately, this promising theme is not fully worked out in the novel. The main thrust of the narrative is the Little People theme, and this is not told with the same masterly control of his 1890s tales. A stunted familiar dogs Hillyer's footsteps, though he cannot see it, and there is a variety of destructive, poltergeist-type activity, but both these devices are too conventional to strike a chord with the reader, and nowhere near as compelling as the shadowy rituals hinted at in the deep forests and hollows of Gwent in 'The Shining Pyramid' and 'The Novel of the Black Seal'. Neither is there any clear correlation between the Little People theme and the otherworld motif, so that the novel does not quite cohere. As a further exploration of the idea of a world which intersects with our own, a spiritual region holding both imperishable delight and fundamental danger, *The Green Round* cannot be entirely disregarded: but as literature it is a failure, with a narrative prolonged by commercial considerations, and a vicarious 'horror' element similarly dictated.

Machen remained in demand as a writer of fine prose throughout the 1930s, but it was mostly private presses that gave him the freedom to choose his own theme. Thus, for the Appelicon Press of Westport, Connecticut, he provided an elegant and erudite essay on the anonymous poem, 'Tom O'Bedlam's Song' (circa 1620), with its suggestive references to goblincraft and a phantom world; for the Rowfant Club of Cleveland, he allowed the reprinting of his letters to an American admirer, Munson Havens; and the Postprandial Press of Georgia issued *The Glitter of the Brook*, a collection of five essays Machen had written for a local paper. Yet he had not quite finished with fiction. Spurred, as he said in a letter to Colin Summerford, by John Gawsworth's success in placing *The Cosy Room*, Machen managed to get a contract with Hutchinson for a volume of new short stories, amounting to 50,000 words, 'but', he continued, 'I am sure that, in the words of Dryden (more or less) you will not, from the dregs of Art, think to receive what the first sprightly running could not give'. He finished the collection in about six months and it was published in September 1936. Although Machen clearly regarded it as hackwork, and a hard thing to expect of a man in his seventies who had already given his life to literature with only middling reward and appreciation, he also seems to have taken some pride in the stories. In a letter to A.E. Waite, he conceded 'I believe you are right in thinking that there are hints or indications of new paths in "The Children of the Pool" — but it is getting very late and dark for treading of strange ways'. It is usual to regard this book as of little consequence.

Joshi calls it 'arid and tired' and is rather donnishly critical of Machen for allowing it to appear. Certainly, Machen was in meagre circumstances, and wrote the stories because he was paid to, and wrote them quickly because he had a deadline to meet and his experience of publishers did not incline him to trust their indulgence too long. But this should not make us presume that he was any the less committed to the prose craft he had perfected over five decades, or the mystical philosophy he had always held.

Of the six stories, two are not supernatural. 'The Bright Boy' tells how a young graduate commissioned as a private tutor to a child prodigy comes to connect the family he serves with a dreadful crime done to a young girl deep in a nearby forest; years later, it emerges the 'child' is a freakish adult whose physical development ceased at seven or eight, and who uses two accomplices to pose as his parents as a mask for his hideous urges. The story is set in Gwent again, and Machen returns to his fascination with Bertholly, the scene of *The Great God Pan*: 'the White House ... stood, terraced on a hill-side, high above a grey and silver river winding in esses through a lonely, lovely valley. Above it, to the east, was a vast and shadowy and ancient wood, climbing to the high ridge of the hill, and descending by height and by depth of green to the level meadows and to the sea ...'. 'The Tree of Life' is also set deep in Gwent, at Llantrisant Abbey, ancestral home of the Teilo Morgans, 'in rich and pleasant meadow-land, with woods of oak and beech and ash and elm all about it. Through the park ran the swift, clear river, Afon Torfaen ... and the hills stood round the Abbey on every side'. Into this idyllic scene, Machen inserts a gentle irony, a story of kindness, and an inheritance mystery all in one, for the squire we see discussing the estate with his steward at the outset turns out to be merely a claimant to the demesne, whose delusions are indulged by the true owner. This is a picturesque tale, rather wry in tone and, while it does not have the radiance of his mystical works, there is still a certain lingering resonance, nor is it unreasonable to see a quiet allegory in play.

'The Exalted Omega' is probably one of the tales Machen had in mind when he spoke of 'new paths'. It is a ghost story (unusually for Machen, who seldom used the traditional spectre in his fiction) but of a curiously indirect kind. We witness a recluse's melancholy and aimless existence in rooms in a London square, and the harsh voices and visions that assail him: we see a fraudulent medium at work, and learn she sometimes seems genuinely possessed; we get hints about a murder which is to take place. Only at the end of the story does it become clear that the latter part of the recluse's existence is as a ghost, so imperceptibly does Machen fade the character out of a futile life and into a continued existence equally futile. That his spirit witnesses a murder plot and tries to warn of this through the low-grade psychic is an almost unnecessary punchline: the desperate fatalism of the recluse is horror enough. 'The Exalted Omega' is reminiscent of a Walter de la Mare story — 'Mr Kempe', 'A Recluse', 'The House', 'The Looking Glass' and others in which the borderline between life and death is blurred. The technique of disguising the full significance of what is shown to the reader had been used by Machen before but much more blatantly, and, all in all, the story is thought-provoking and a worthwhile addition to the

Machen canon.

The remaining three stories are in more familiar Machen terrain. In 'Out of the Picture', Machen reverts to the Jekyll and Hyde theme that recurs in his fiction (for example, 'The Novel of the White Powder', 'Psychology') in telling of an artist whose landscapes in the eighteenth century manner have a mood of 'oppression and terror' and invariably feature a twisted, sinister figure. When a series of violent crimes occurs in the area around the artist's studio, and the artist disappears, we are left to draw our own inferences as to the significance of this figure. 'Change' is an effective return to the theme of the malignant Little People, with a young governess who has something about her of Helen in *The Great God Pan*, the girl in 'The White People' and Miss Lally of *The Three Impostors*, a dark and alluring villainess who is both victim and votary of the rites of these primal creatures. Only the title story of this collection does not quite come off. In 'The Children of the Pool', the narrator, returning to Gwent, finds an old acquaintance staying in a cottage by a dank and shadowed pond. The acquaintance is tormented by voices that taunt him about a mild indiscretion of years ago. Machen attempts to demonstrate that the landscape, in particular the evil-looking pool, could have called forth morbid delusions, but the explanation is unconvincing and the argument putting this notion forward is overlong. This is the only real failure in the book, though, and 'The Tree of Life', 'The Exalted Omega' and 'Change' all deserve better credit than they tend to be given.

Machen's status as a venerable man of letters who had devoted a lifetime to literature as a sacred craft, not merely a profession, received some recognition in his twilight years. The circle of younger writers who admired his work — Oliver Stonor, Frank Baker, Norah Hoult, Colin Summerford, Sylvia Townsend Warner, Faith Compton Mackenzie and others — were instrumental in getting him a modest Civil List pension in 1933, while in 1937 he was honoured with a civic luncheon in his home county of Monmouthshire/Gwent, and in 1943 an Appeal Fund, supported by many notable literary figures, including T.S. Eliot, Bernard Shaw, Siegfried Sassoon, Max Beerholm and Walter de la Mare, raised enough to keep the Machens in tolerable comfort for the remainder of their days. The Fund culminated in an eightieth birthday dinner attended by many of the eminent contributors, at which Machen was finally accorded the respect he might have thought would never be his.

Yet he had not quite finished with literature. A project he had long had in mind came to fruition in 1941 when Constable commissioned him to edit and introduce *A Handy Dickens*. The prefaces he wrote for books written by two fellow Monmouthshire writers find him still fervent in the assertion of the spiritual reality of things, and in the particular quality of the Gwent countryside as a demonstration of this. For W. Townsend Collins' *The Romance of the Echoing Wood* (1937), he quoted again the saying of the alchemist Oswald Crollius, 'In every grain of wheat there lies hidden the soul of a star', and reminded readers: 'The grain of wheat ... discloses undreamed of wonders: much more does the whole world and sum of things, the spiritual world of men and all their works, disclose incredible but most veracious marvels to those who gaze on it in the spirit of romance'. And for Fred J. Hando's *The Pleasant Land of Gwent* (1944) he scans again, across the years, his memories of the old country, and his attempts to transmute what he felt for his land into the highest prose: 'I have tried here and there to make the page utter the awe and delight with which, by hills and woods, by deep, ferny overshadowed lanes, I first came from Llanddewi Rectory to the level of Tredonoc, and there saw, at a turn of the road, suddenly, in a moment: Wentwood, green, great and exalted; the silvery winding of the river, and the vast peace of the still valley'.

Just as it was appropriate that one of his last pieces of writing should celebrate again the Gwent of his childhood, so was it fitting that his final substantial work on his own account should return to the other great love of his childhood: literature. In 1943 Frank Baker arranged for him to contribute an essay to a young, traditionalist journal, *The Wind and the Rain*. Machen's essay, modestly entitled 'A Note on Poetry', is a reiteration and summation of the assertions on the essence of literature he gave in *Hieroglyphics* forty years earlier: it is a reaffirmation, too, of the supreme significance of art and spirituality for humanity. Calling upon Milton, Poe, Keats and Shelley as allies, Machen summons again a vision of an otherworld to which the sublimity and beauty of the finest poetry owes its origin — Keats' 'faery lands forlorn', Shelley's evocation of 'the eternal, which must glow/Through time and change, unquenchably the same':

> ...there is in the human consciousness, as it were a space or tract which is sensitive to the approach and presence of poetry

and painting, of music and architecture, to that dim, uncon-
jectured region whence all these arise: in fine, to the arts. This
tract is utterly independent of the logical understanding, of
common sense, and of reason — in the popular, and not the
Coleridgean significance of the word. This territory, with
poetry and the other arts which flourish in it, is not merely of
the nature of man, it is man, it is that which makes man to be
what he is. Its presence in the consciousness is that which
differences men from pig, however learned the pig may be. If
this tract must have a name, perhaps it should be styled
Wonder: though Coleridge, in 'Kubla Khan', calls it Xanadu.

Arthur Machen died in 1947, a few months after his wife Purefoy.
The writer chided by a critic for his insistence on 'Latin tags' but
revered by many for his allegiance to a faith founded on the celebration of the ineffable, has carved on his gravestone in Old Amersham
cemetery:

OMNIA EXEUNT IN MYSTERIUM

Eight: Conclusion

How has Arthur Machen's work survived in the fifty years since he wrote his last pieces? In the year before he died, Penguin Books issued a paperback selection from his short stories. Although this was mostly drawn from weaker work, such as the later stories and the wartime legends, it achieved a popular success such as Machen could scarcely have thought possible. He told Oliver Stonor gleefully that on account of the title, *Holy Terrors*, 'the happy purchaser will think himself in for an hour's wholesome fun, in a tale concerned with the doings of some very bad children' but added, 'I have no cry here: these Penguins have built up a momentum: a sale of Eighty-three Thousand hath a noble sound'. The momentum continued after his death with the issue of a stronger anthology, *Tales of Horror and the Supernatural*, in America (1948) and Britain (1949), with a fine introduction by Philip Van Doren Stern in which he continues the stance of earlier American critics who liked to present Machen's writing as if it were the preserve of some secret cult to which admittance was only for a discerning élite: 'A taste for his work has to be acquired;' he warned, 'the writing is polished and elaborate, the thinking is subtle, and the imagery is rich with the glowing colour that is to be found in medieval church glass. His style does not belong to our period of stripped diction and fast-moving prose...'. *The Hill of Dreams* was reprinted in 1954, with a new introduction, which was amongst the last writings of that great fantasist Lord Dunsany, paying tribute to Machen's dedication to the cause of fine literature despite the hardships he endured, and asking, rhetorically: 'Is there anything more in literature than seeing one's vision and remaining true to it, and then putting it on to paper clearly and beautifully?'.

The centenary of Machen's birth, 1963, was celebrated with a wireless broadcast, *Remembering Arthur Machen*, edited by Frank

Baker, with contributions from Machen's son Hilary and daughter Janet, writers Sylvia Townsend Warner, Morchard Bishop and Nora Hoult, and other friends. Reynolds and Charlton's biography appeared in the same year, and the early sixties also saw an American-based Machen Society active.

There was an explosion of interest in fantasy writing in the mid to late sixties and early seventies, lead by the revival of J.R.R. Tolkien's *Lord of the Rings*, and Machen's work, including *The Hill of Dreams* and the supernatural stories, found paperback editions. His work has been cited as an influence by several songwriters in the pop culture and folk music idioms of this period.

After a brief lean period, during which virtually all of his work fell out of print, the late eighties saw a strong renewal, with the formation of a new Machen Society based in his home town of Caerleon, the publication of his *Selected Letters* (1988) and an omnibus volume, *The Collected Arthur Machen*, in the same year. Further paperback editions of *The Hill of Dreams* and *The Great God Pan*, together with a host of private press editions of his scarcer work, have continued this present epiphany, now sustained for over a decade. Russian, Japanese, German, Italian, Spanish and other translations of his work have appeared. As Ferdinand Mount, now editor of the *Times Literary Supplement*, has observed, 'Machen keeps on popping up':

> ... one can trace lines of descent from Machen in all sorts of directions — though Crowley and the GD (Golden Dawn) to Crowley's young disciple, L. Ron Hubbard, who was to evolve ... 'scientology'; through the hippies and the Alternative Culture to the revival of interest in prehistoric magic and the numinosity of standing stones and ley lines; through artists like Sutherland and Ceri Richards, to the Neo-Romantic art of thorn-thicket and hollow lanes, and so on, in an infinite diversity of religious and nationalist enthusiasms, all variously in revolt against the modern world ...
> (*The Spectator*, 29 October 1988)

Machen's work had a profound influence on the composer John Ireland (1879-1962) who dedicated his Legend, for Piano and Orchestra to him: it was in part inspired by an apparent sighting of dancing children in old costume who vanished in a moment. When Ireland told Machen what he had seen, the writer's postcard reply was brief: 'So you have seen them too'. The music critic Christopher

Palmer has described Ireland's encounter with Machen's work as 'life-changing'. The film director Michael Powell (1905-90) had a similar experience at the age of twenty when introduced to Machen's books by Rex Ingram, with whom he was learning the art of film. At the end of his life, Powell wrote: 'It is fitting that I record now, many years later, in 1988, how much I owe to him for terror, pity and fantasy — how much we all owe to the Wizard of Gwent' (MS, 15 1988). Machen's work had the same lasting impact on the American author Paul Bowles who read him as a youth. His biographer Christopher Sawyer-Laucanno records that Machen's books 'would remain in Paul's memory for a long time, with the themes markedly re-echoing in some of his later fiction' (*An Invisible Spectator, A Biography of Paul Bowles*, 1989, 38).

Machen has remained a towering figure in the separate world of horror and supernatural fiction, where he is routinely classed as one of the masters, usually in company with J. Sheridan Le Fanu, M.R. James, Algernon Blackwood and H.P. Lovecraft. Modern exponents in this field such as Stephen King, Clive Barker and Ramsey Campbell have all acknowledged Machen's authority and influence and at least two novels have been written as deliberate developments of Machen's fiction: Gerald Suster's *The Devil's Maze* (1979), a pastiche of *The Three Impostors*, and T.E.D. Klein's *The Ceremonies* (1984) which draws on Machen's 'The White People'. Some thematic debt can also be discerned in the earlier supernatural thrillers of Charles Williams.

Yet it is not only on creative artists that Machen's work has exercised influence. His strong, lifelong faith in the absolute reality of a world beyond this one, infinitely more profound and potentially perilous, and his understanding of the possibility of some tantalising connections with the mundane world, have led some to regard him highly as a visionary. Evelyn Underhill (1875-1941), the author of *Mysticism* (1911), still recognised as an authoritative work on the subject, met Machen when they were both members of one of A.E. Waite's occult orders, and dedicated her novel *The Column of Dust* (1909) to Machen and Purefoy. Wesley Sweetser has observed that some passages in *Mysticism* are virtually paraphrases or distillations of episodes in Machen's writings, and he speculates that Machen may have unofficially edited the book. The lurid early horror stories have probably stopped his later, more spiritually-charged work, such as *A Fragment of Life* and *The Secret Glory*, from receiving appropriate attention from students of mysticism, but his peculiarly personal and vivid recharging of a form of Neoplatonism, if never fully expressed, is worth pursuing: a chapbook garnering the quintessence of his beliefs could commend itself as a spiritual classic.

In the study of Anglo-Welsh literature, Machen has seldom received his due. He was undeniably proud of his Welshness and more usually referred to his home county as Gwent even though its official designation during his lifetime was the English name, Monmouthshire (it became Gwent to the bureaucrats in the local government changes made in the 1970s). He was a close friend of Caradoc Evans whom he described as 'very turbulent, highly entertaining' and delightedly recalled an occasion when the two of them exchanged a few pleasantries in Welsh in a London pub to the suspicion of the war-wary customers, who imagined they were speaking German: the impression was assisted by another companion who intoned 'Intern them all! Intern them all!' at intervals. Machen admired Evans's writings, and contributed to a memorial volume for him, while Evans supplied the Welsh phrases in Machen's novel *The Great Return*, although according to Machen they were not entirely accurate. Evans's blunt, sinewy writing is on the face of it far removed from Machen's lyrical, romantic prose, but they both had a sharp eye for satire and for the essentially Celtic in character, together with a robust sense of humour.

Perhaps Machen's nearest Welsh literary contemporary was Ernest Rhys (1859-1946), now remembered mainly as the editor for over forty years of Dent's Everyman's Library of pocket classics. But Rhys was also a founder, with Yeats, of the Rhymers' Club, where most of the great nineties poets went, and a writer of Celtic verses such as *Welsh Ballads* (1898) and of Arthurian plays and lyrics, including *The Masque of the Grail* (1908). He was regarded by Yeats as representing Welsh literature in the great Celtic revival of the period. He came from a Carmarthen family, though brought up in Tyneside.

J. Kimberley Roberts (ER 64 1983) has drawn attention to Rhys's London-based view of Wales as 'a kind of Innisfree', Yeats's island sanctuary always 'in the deep heart's core', a sacred pastoral realm. Machen's vision of Gwent in *A Fragment of Life* and *The Secret Glory* is very similar. It is a domain of high mystic importance to the clerk and the schoolboy of these novels, who, exiled from their native land, come to regard it as Yeats regarded Innisfree, an Avalon of the soul. This misty and romantic vision of Wales may not commend itself to many today: but it is one truth. And Machen did not confuse the ideal with the reality.

Though they seem to have met only once, Rhys included Machen in his collection of correspondence from eminent authors, *Letters from Limbo* (1936), in which Machen laments the decline of his beloved Caerleon-on-Usk, 'an agonising spectacle ... It has a training college, three stink factories, and a madhouse ... It is, in fact, as a man told me, "a progressive little place". It is, indeed, it progresses swiftly to *uffern du'* (275). Rhys notes, perceptively, that Machen was 'a humorist as well as a dealer in the mysterious and the occult, with a Celtic strain that comes of his Welsh upbringing'. *Uffern du*, he explains, is Welsh for 'black hell'. Machen did not, in fact, speak Welsh, except for an occasional tag or two, but he was deeply steeped in Welsh hagiography, history and legend, and his revitalising of the images and motifs of these ancient national sources, especially in the Grail novels and essays, has not been properly recognised. Probably few Welsh or Celtic writers have made as much use of their mythological heritage as Machen, and one would have to look to the poet and artist David Jones (1895-1974) or to Yeats for a comparable intensity of inspiration from such deep sources. No history of literature in Wales would be complete without its chapter on Arthur Machen.

Yet, despite the survival of his work in print, the avowed influence he has had on an impressive array of artists and writers, the esteem he earned from major literary figures such as T.S. Eliot, D.H. Lawrence, Henry Miller and Jorge Luis Borges, and the devotion of his followers, Machen remains outside of the literary mainstream. Partly this is due to critical fashion. Machen is a traditionalist when the avant-garde has been in the ascendant; a mystic and ritualist when existentialist humanism is the vogue; a Romantic when kitchen-sink realism is called for; a rhapsodiser of beauty when ugliness is more eagerly worshipped. Perhaps, as some of his qualities come to be valued again, Machen's work may begin to attract wider scholarly interest. But it is more likely that he will always belong with those other individualist writers, such as John Cowper Powys, Henry Williamson, L.H. Myers, and David Lindsay, not afraid to place their own deeply-held form of spirituality at the heart of their work, and trust to certain like souls through the ages to keep it eternal.

Select Bibliography

Place of publication London unless indicated. First and, where appropriate, latest editions only are cited. Translations are omitted. The abbreviations used to refer to these works in the text appear in parentheses.

Primary Sources — The Works of Arthur Machen

Eleusinia, Hereford: 1881; Rhode Island, USA: Necronomicon Press, 1988.
The Anatomy of Tobacco, George Redway, 1884.
Don Quijote de la Mancha, George Redway, 1887.
The Chronicle of Clemendy, privately printed, 1888.
Thesaurus Incantatus, privately printed, 1888.
The Great God Pan, and *The Inmost Light*: John Lane, 1894; Creation 1993.
The Three Impostors, John Lane, 1895.
Hieroglyphics, Grant Richards, 1906.
The House of Souls, Grant Richards, 1906.
Dr Stiggins, Francis Griffiths, 1906.
The Hill of Dreams, Grant Richards, 1907; Dover, New York, 1986.
The Bowmen, and Other Legends of the War, Kent: Simpkin, Marshall, Hamilton, 1915.
The Great Return, The Faith Press, 1915.
The Terror, Duckworth, 1917.
War and the Christian Faith, Skeffington, 1918.
The Secret Glory, Martin Secker, 1922.
Far Off Things, Martin Secker, 1922.
Things Near and Far, Martin Secker, 1923. (TNF)
The Grande Trouvaille, First Edition Bookshop, 1923.
The Shining Pyramid, Chicago, USA: Covici-McGee, 1923.

The Collector's Craft, First Edition Bookshop, 1923.
Strange Roads, The Classic Press, 1923; Caerleon: Green Round Press, 1990.
Dog and Duck, Jonathan Cape, 1924.
The London Adventure, Martin Secker, 1924.
The Glorious Mystery, Chicago: Covici-McGee, 1924.
Precious Balms, Spurr and Swift, 1924.
Ornaments in Jade, New York: Knopf, 1924.
The Shining Pyramid, Martin Secker, 1925 (differs from the USA edition).
The Canning Wonder, Chatto and Windus, 1925.
Dreads and Drolls, Martin Secker, 1926.
Notes and Queries, Spurr and Swift, 1926.
Tom O'Bedlam And His Song, Connecticut: Apellicon Press, 1930.
A Few Letters, Cleveland, Ohio: The Rowfant Club, 1932; Cheshire: Aylesford Press,1993. (AFL)
The Green Round, Ernest Benn, 1933.
The Cosy Room, Rich and Cowan, 1936.
The Children of the Pool, Hutchinson, 1936; Salem: Ayer, 1987.
Holy Terrors, Harmondsworth: Penguin, 1946.
Bridles and Spurs, Cleveland: The Rowfant Club, 1951.
Guinevere and Lancelot and Others, Newport News, USA: Purple Mouth Press, 1986.
The Collected Arthur Machen, Duckworth, 1988.
The Secret Glory, Chapters Five and Six, Lewes: Tartarus Press, 1991.
The Day's Portion, An Arthur Machen Miscellany, Pontypool: Village Publishing, 1991.
Rus in Urbe And Other Pieces, Lewes: Tartarus Press, 1992.
Ritual And Other Stories, Lewes: Tartarus Press, 1992.
The Secret of the Sangraal, Horam, East Sussex: Tartarus Press, 1995. (SS)

Secondary Sources

Adcock, A. St John. *The Glory That Was Grub Street*, Sampson Low, 1928. (ASA)
Avallaunius, the Journal of the Arthur Machen Society, 19 Cross Street, Caerleon, Gwent, NP6 1AF. (AV)
Baker, Frank. *I Follow But Myself*, Peter Davies, 1968. (FB)

BIBLIOGRAPHY

Bantock, Raymond. *A Book of Poems in Prose*. Tokyo: Bummei-Shoin, 1925. (RB)

Betjeman, John. *Summoned By Bells*, John Murphy, 1960.

Bleiler, E.F.. *The Guide to Supernatural Fiction*, Ohio: Kent State University Press, 1983. (EFB)

Burke, Thomas. *Son of London*. Herbert Jenkins, 1947. (TB)

Danielson, Henry. *Arthur Machen: A Bibliography*, the author, 1923.

Dobson, Roger; Brangham, Godfrey; and Gilbert, R.A.. *Arthur Machen, Selected Letters*, Wellingborough: Aquarian Press, 1988. (SL)

Dowling, Linda. *Language and Decadence in the Victorian Fin de Siècle*, Princeton University Press, 1986.

Ellmann, Richard. *Oscar Wilde*, Hamish Hamilton, 1987.

Gilbert, R.A., *A.E. Waite*, Crucible, Wellingborough, 1987 (RAG)

Goldstone, Adrian and Sweetser, Wesley. *A Bibliography of Arthur Machen*, Austin: University of Texas Press, 1965.

Jerome, Jerome K. *My Life and Times*, Hodder & Stoughton, 1926. (JKJ)

Jordan-Smith, Paul. *On Strange Altars*, Brentano's, 1923. (PJS)

Joshi, S.T. *The Weird Tale*, Austin: University of Texas Press, 1990. (SJ)

McClure, Kevin. *Visions of Bowmen and Angels*, the author, 1993.

Machen, Purefoy. *Where Memory Slept*, Caerleon: Green Round, 1991. (PM)

Merrill, Stuart. *Pastels in Prose*, New York: Harpers, 1890. (PIP)

Michael, D.P.M.. *Arthur Machen*, Cardiff: University of Wales Press, 1971. (DPM)

Punter, David. *The Literature of Terror, A History of Gothic Fictions from 1765 to the Present Day*, Longman, 1980. (LT)

Reynolds, Aidan and Charlton, William. *Arthur Machen, A Biography*, Richards Press, 1963; Oxford: Caermaen, 1988. (RC)

Roberts, J. Kimberly. *Ernest Rhys*. Cardiff: University of Wales Press, 1983. (ER)

Russell, R.B.. *Machenalia* (two volumes), Lewes: Tartarus Press, 1990.

Savage, Henry. *Richard Middleton*, Cecil Palmer, 1922.

Society of Young Men in Spectacles. *Machenstruck*, Oxford: Caermaen, 1988. (MS)

Starrett, Vincent. *Arthur Machen, A Novelist of Ecstasy and Sin*, Chicago: Walter M. Hill, 1918. (VS)

(Starrett, Vincent). *Starrett vs. Machen, A record of discovery and correspondence*, St Louis: Autolycus Press, 1977. (SM)

Stock, A.G.. *W.B. Yeats: His Poetry and Thought*, Cambridge University Press, 1961. (AGS)

Sullivan, Jack (ed.). *The Penguin Encyclopedia of Horror and the Supernatural*, Harmondsworth: Viking Penguin, 1986. (PEHS)

Sweetser, Wesley. *Arthur Machen*, New York: Grosset and Dunlap, 1964. (WS)

Valentine, Mark and Dobson, Roger. *Arthur Machen, Artist and Mystic*, Oxford: Caermaen, 1986. (A & M)

Yeats, W.B. *Autobiographies*, Macmillan, 1955.

Acknowledgements

I would like to record my grateful acknowledgements to the following: firstly, Rita Tait of the Arthur Machen Society, who played an important part in making this book possible; Janet Pollock, Arthur Machen's daughter; Roger Dobson, for his particular help, Ray Russell, Godfrey Brangham, Jon Preece, Graham Cooling, Paul Beveridge, Colin and Joan Langeveld, Jeff Dempsey, David Cowperthwaite, Ron Weighell, Marie Procter; John Powell Ward, editor of the Border Lines series, for his unfailing patience and courtesy; and, most of all, Debbie: she knows why.

Thanks are also due to Taits Gallery for illustrations 2, 3, 4 and 5, and to the Arthur Machen Society for illustrations 1, 7, 8, 9, 10.

Series Afterword

The Border country is that region between England and Wales which is upland and lowland, both and neither. Centuries ago kings and barons fought over these Marches without their national allegiance ever being settled. In our own time, referring to his childhood, that eminent borderman Raymond Williams once said 'We talked of "The English" who were not us, and "The Welsh" who were not us'. It is beautiful, gentle, intriguing and often surprising. It displays majestic landscapes, which show a lot, and hide some more. People now walk it, poke into its cathedrals and bookshops, and fly over or hang-glide from its mountains, yet its mystery remains.

In cultural terms the region is as fertile as (in parts) its agriculture and soil. The continued success of the Three Choirs Festival and the growth of the border town of Hay as a centre of the second-hand book trade have both attracted international recognition. The present series of introductory books is offered in the light of such events. Writers as diverse as Mary Webb, Raymond Williams and Wilfred Owen are seen in the special light — perhaps that cloudy golden twilight so characteristic of the region — of their origin in this area or association with it. There are titles too, though fewer, on musicians and painters. The Gloucestershire composers such as Samuel Sebastian Wesley, and painters like David Jones, bear an imprint of border woods, rivers, villages and hills.

How wide is the border? Two, five or fifteen miles each side of the boundary; it depends on your perspective, on the placing of the nearest towns, on the terrain itself, and on history. In the time of Offa and after, Hereford itself was a frontier town, and Welsh was spoken there even in the nineteenth century. True border folk traditionally did not recognise those from even a few miles away. Today, with greater mobility, the crossing of boundaries is easier, whether for education, marriage, art or leisure. For myself, who spent some

144

childhood years in Herefordshire and a decade of middle age crossing between England and Wales once a week, I can only say that as
you approach the border you feel it. Suddenly you are in that finally
elusive terrain, looking from a bare height down onto the plain, or
from lower land up to a gap in the hills, and you want to explore it,
maybe not to return.

This elusiveness pertains to the writers and artists too. It is often
difficult to decide who is border, to what extent and with what
impact on their work. The urbane Elizabeth Barrett Browning,
prominent figure of the salons of London and Italy in her time, spent
virtually all her life until her late twenties outside Ledbury in
Herefordshire, and this fact is being seen by current critics and
scholars as of more and more significance. The twentieth century
'English pastoral' composers — with names like Parry, Howells and
Vaughan Williams — were nearly all border people. One wonders
whether border country is now suddenly found on the English side
of the Severn Bridge, and how far even John Milton's *Comus*, famous
for its first production in Ludlow Castle, is in any sense such a work.
Then there is the fascinating Uxbridge-born Peggy Eileen Whistler,
transposed in the 1930s into Margiad Evans to write her (epilepsis-
based) visionary novels set near her adored Ross-on-Wye and which
today still retain a magical charm. Further north: could Barbara Pym,
born and raised in Oswestry, even remotely be called a border
writer? Most people would say that the poet A.E. Housman was far
more so, yet he hardly visited the county after which his chief book
of poems, *A Shropshire Lad*, is named. Further north still: there is the
village of Chirk on the boundary itself, where R.S. Thomas had his
first curacy; there is Gladstone's Hawarden Library, just outside
Chester and actually into Clwyd in Wales itself; there is intriguingly
the Wirral town of Birkenhead, where Wilfred Owen spent his
adolescence and where his fellow war poet Hedd Wyn was awarded
his Chair — posthumously.

On the Welsh side the names are different. The mystic Ann
Griffiths; the metaphysical poet Henry Vaughan; the astonishing
nineteenth century symbolist novelist Arthur Machen (in Linda
Dowling's phrase, 'Pater's prose as registered by Wilde'); and the
remarkable Thomas Olivers of Gregynog, associated with the writing of the well-known hymn 'Lo He comes with clouds descending'.
Those descending clouds ...; in border country the scene hangs
overhead, and it is easy to indulge in unwarranted speculation. Most

145

significant perhaps is the difference between the two peoples on either side. From England, the border meant the enticement of emptiness, a strange unpopulated land, going up and up into the hills. From Wales, the border meant the road to London, to the university, or to employment, whether by droving sheep, or later to the industries of Birmingham and Liverpool. It also meant the enemy, since borders and boundaries are necessarily political. Much is shared, yet different languages are spoken, in more than one sense.

With certain notable exceptions, the books in this series are short introductory studies of one person's work or some aspect of it. There are normally no indexes. The bibliography lists main sources referred to in the text and sometimes others, for those who would like to pursue the topic further. The authors reflect the diversity of their subjects. They are specialists or academics; critics or biographers; poets or musicians themselves; or ordinary people with, however, an established reputation of writing imaginatively and directly about what moves them. They are of various ages, both sexes, Welsh and English, border people themselves or from further afield.

To those who explore the matter, the subjects — the writers, painters and composers written about — seem increasingly united by a particular kind of vision. This holds good however diverse they are in other, main ways; and of course they are diverse indeed. One might scarcely associate, it would seem, Raymond Williams with Samuel Sebastian Wesley, or Dennis Potter with Thomas Traherne. But one has to be careful in such assumptions. The epigraph to Bruce Chatwin's twentieth century novel *On the Black Hill* is a passage from the seventeenth century mystic writer Jeremy Taylor. Thomas Traherne himself is the subject of a recent American study which puts Traherne's writings into dialogue with European philosopher-critics like Martin Heidegger, Jacques Derrida and Jacques Lacan. And a current best-selling writer of thrillers, Ellis Peters, sets her stories in a Shrewsbury of the late medieval Church with a cunning quiet monk as her ever-engaging sleuth.

The vision (name incidentally of the farmhouse in Chatwin's novel) is something to do with the curious border light already mentioned. To avoid getting sentimental and mystic here — though border writers have sometimes been both — one might suggest that this effect is meteorological. Perhaps the sun's rays are refracted through skeins of dew and mist that hit the stark mountains and low hills at curious ascertainable angles, with prismatic results. Not that rainbows are the point in our area: it is more the contrasts of gold, green and grey. Some writers never mention it. They don't have to. But all the artists of the region see it, are affected by it, and transpose their highly different emanations of reality through its transparencies. Meanwhile, on the ground, the tourist attractions draw squads from diverse cultural and ethnic origins; agriculture enters the genetic-engineering age; New Age travellers are welcome and unwelcome; and the motorway runs up parallel past all — 'Lord of the M5', as the poet Geoffrey Hill has dubbed the Saxon king Offa, he of the dyke which bisects the region where it can still be identified. The region has its uniqueness, then, and a statistically above-average number of writers and artists (we have identified over fifty clear candidates so far) have drawn something from it, which it is the business of the present series to elucidate.

The admirable Arthur Machen's relative neglect since his death generates a defensive itch to list the luminaries who have praised his work. They include George Moore, W.B. Yeats, Oscar Wilde, H.G. Wells, Siegfried Sassoon, John Betjeman, composer John Ireland, film-maker Michael Powell, cellist Julian Lloyd Webber, TV personality Barry Humphries, and numerous pop musicians and science-fiction writers. And there are signs of an upturn to what Mark Valentine calls the 'reappraisal'; he pointedly notes a remark of Ferdinand Mount as recently as 1988, that 'Machen keeps on popping up'. More lately still have come the diaries of Sylvia Townsend Warner (niece by marriage), while Bill Bryden's play *The Big Picnic*, set in World War I and featuring the Mons Angels story, was recently produced in Glasgow. Some of our society's current preoccupations — *fin-de-siècle*, green landscapes and horror — suggest that we need Machen back again. Mark Valentine's detailed and vivid study provides an opportunity.

John Powell Ward